A fresh sense of awe spread through him

His child.

With an effort, Owen remembered why they'd come to the examination room. "Move it some more," he said. Bailey shifted the device, and they both heard the same thing.

Another galloping horse in the background. "Could that be an echo?" Bailey asked.

Enough of halfway measures. "Let's find out for sure," Owen said, and, after removing the stethoscope, switched on the sonogram machine.

His gut tightened. Because for just a moment, in the rush of noises, he'd imagined he heard a little voice whispering, "Hello, Daddy."

Or had that been two little voices?

Dear Reader,

While each book in the Safe Harbor Medical miniseries stands on its own, I like to include secondary characters and situations that readers can enjoy following. In earlier books, we prepared for the arrival of the brilliant but arrogant surgeon Dr. Owen Tartikoff, head of the hospital's new fertility program. We also met bubbly, offbeat nurse Bailey Wayne, who agreed to become a surrogate mother for her sister.

Both of these characters have surprises in store for them. One of them is that Owen's half brother, Boone, is married to Bailey's older sister. Also, there's an unexpected twist to the surrogacy. Several, in fact.

To add to the fun, I decided to force these two opposite characters to share a house. Bailey's not the type to let herself be pushed around, even by a man who wields so much power at work. As for Owen, he has some important life lessons to learn, such as how to share a bathroom with a woman who insists on dominating the counter space.

This strong-willed duo is embarking on a journey of self-discovery. It's great to have you with us, so please fasten your seat belt and let's go!

Best,

Jacqueline Diamond

The Surgeon's Surprise Twins

JACQUELINE DIAMOND

TORONTO NEW YORK LONDON
AMSTERDAM PARIS SYDNEY HAMBURG
STOCKHOLM ATHENS TOKYO MILAN MADRID
PRAGUE WARSAW BUDAPEST AUCKLAND

Recycling programs
for this product may
not exist in your area.

ISBN-13: 978-0-373-75379-6

THE SURGEON'S SURPRISE TWINS

Copyright © 2011 by Jackie Hyman

All rights reserved. Except for use in any review, the reproduction or
utilization of this work in whole or in part in any form by any electronic,
mechanical or other means, now known or hereafter invented, including
xerography, photocopying and recording, or in any information storage
or retrieval system, is forbidden without the written permission of the
publisher, Harlequin Enterprises Limited, 225 Duncan Mill Road,
Don Mills, Ontario M3B 3K9, Canada.

This is a work of fiction. Names, characters, places and incidents are
either the product of the author's imagination or are used fictitiously,
and any resemblance to actual persons, living or dead, business
establishments, events or locales is entirely coincidental.

This edition published by arrangement with Harlequin Books S.A.

For questions and comments about the quality of this book
please contact us at Customer_eCare@Harlequin.ca

® and TM are trademarks of the publisher. Trademarks indicated with
® are registered in the United States Patent and Trademark Office, the
Canadian Trade Marks Office and in other countries.

www.Harlequin.com

Printed in U.S.A.

ABOUT THE AUTHOR

Medical issues and police work are areas that fascinate Jacqueline Diamond, who's written more than eighty-five romances and mysteries. A former reporter and editor for two newspapers and the Associated Press, Jackie researches her subjects on the internet and with the help of friends who are professionals in the fields. As for family relationships, she does her research the old-fashioned way, through experience and observation. Jackie, who received a career achievement award from *RT Book Reviews*, lives in Orange County, California, with her husband, Kurt. She hopes you'll visit her website at www.jacquelinediamond.com to get the latest on her books and writing tips.

Books by Jacqueline Diamond

‡Downhome Doctors
*Harmony Circle
**Safe Harbor Medical

Chapter One

Dr. Owen Tartikoff adjusted his designer sunglasses against the glare of the July sun reflecting off the Mediterranean-style mansion. He had to admit that his half brother's harborside house looked impressive, but that didn't explain Owen's need to take a couple of deep breaths of sea air to calm his nerves.

He was about to meet the most important person in his life. He'd had no idea it would feel this way. Made no sense, really. The person hadn't even been born yet.

He took a moment to survey his surroundings. Beyond the mansion lay the marina that gave the town of Safe Harbor, California, its name. Row after row of yachts and other boats lay at anchor. At noon on a Friday, only a few sailboats dotted the water.

This place must be worth millions. He was glad to see Boone and his wife, Phyllis, doing so well with their investment firm.

Pushing his thoughts aside, Owen strode up the mosaic tile walkway to the carved double doors and pressed the bell. Chimes echoed through what sounded like a cathedral. Then he waited. When no one answered, he rang again.

At last, the slap of sandals inside announced a woman's approach. He braced himself. What did you say in a situation like this, anyway? Congratulations? Thanks? Or did you pretend you didn't notice?

The door opened to show a tumble of golden-blond curls and a surprised expression. His sister-in-law—who had been a brunette the last time he saw her, a couple of years ago—blinked rapidly before finding her voice. "Owen!"

"Boone did tell you I was stopping by to pick up the key, didn't he?" As an afterthought, Owen put in, "Sorry I haven't come by sooner, but this past week's been crazy."

"I understand." She stepped back, ushering him into an elegant foyer. Marble floor, peach-colored walls, Persian carpet, a mirror in a gilded frame.

Owen didn't care about the decor. He cared about the fact that, in a bare-midriff outfit that showed off her slim waistline, Phyllis Storey was obviously not three months pregnant.

With his baby. Or anyone else's. That troubled Owen more than he would have believed.

"Boone told me…" He broke off. As one of the country's leading fertility specialists, Owen knew what a painful topic miscarriage was for a woman, and he didn't want to press her on the subject. But his sister-in-law was standing there with her head cocked, awaiting clarification, so he continued. "When I called a couple of months ago, Boone mentioned a due date in January."

Her mouth formed an O. "He didn't tell you we'd arranged for a surrogate?"

Gee, he left that part out. Come to think of it, Boone had bragged about the pregnancy at the start of the call, then dropped the subject once he learned his kid brother was moving out from Boston to head the new fertility program at Safe Harbor Medical Center. Boone must have assumed initially that Owen would never find out that his genetic donation hadn't gone directly to Phyllis.

A surrogate. Owen hoped they'd chosen the woman wisely. But that wasn't really his business, was it?

He felt a not-unfamiliar urge to go shake his sibling, whose deep voice he could hear faintly from a distant room. Growing up, Owen had idolized his eight years older half brother, but gradually he'd realized that Boone had his quirks. For one thing, he never told others more than was absolutely necessary, about anything.

"I wish he'd trust me more," Owen grumbled. "I was happy to help you have a baby, by whatever means necessary." He'd proved that by sending several donations, as needed, via medical courier.

"You've been wonderful." Phyllis gave him a million-watt smile. She'd been an actress and model before marrying his brother, and at age forty, hadn't lost her sparkle. "I'm delighted you're going to be living close by. Family's important."

"Yes, it is." Another thought occurred to him. "This surrogate—did you arrange for her through Safe Harbor?" Although the fertility program wouldn't officially open until September, the hospital had a number of obstetrician-gynecologists already on staff.

She tugged on the silvery bracelets piled along one slender arm. "We're using a clinic in L.A., remember?" That was roughly an hour's drive to the north.

"Oh, of course." That *was* where he'd sent his specimens. Still, Owen wished they'd decided to switch to a facility closer to home. He'd have liked to watch the pregnancy progress, just to make sure everything went as it should. "Well, congratulations."

His brother's voice grew louder, angrier. He must be on the phone, since no one seemed to be arguing back.

A vague gesture set Phyllis's bracelets jangling. "We

have a major financial deal pending. You know how that goes."

Actually, Owen didn't. What money he'd saved after paying off his medical school bills was stashed in a bank, a mutual fund and half ownership in a house. Which brought him to the subject at hand. "About the key."

"The key?" she repeated.

"Boone promised to drop it off at my hotel. Apparently he forgot. My furniture arrives Monday and I'd like to figure out where to arrange things." The renter had recently moved out of the house Owen co-owned with Boone. That was convenient, since Owen had a lot more important things to do than search for a place to live.

"Which, um…?"

"I'll take care of it. Just point me toward my brother."

"This way." Phyllis scurried through one of several doorways opening off the foyer, and Owen followed. They passed an ornate living room full of silk-covered sofas, carved and glass-topped tables, and niches set with Greek-style sculptures.

"Nice place," he said.

"We like it." Again, that high-wattage smile. "Here you go."

Through an arched opening, they entered a large room with a spectacular view of the harbor. Judging by the array of printers, computers, file cabinets and fax machines, this was not only a home office but also the center of their business. On the wall hung an artist's rendering of what appeared to be a resort development.

From behind a vast desk, Boone glanced their way. At the sight of them, his brooding expression yielded instantly to a broad smile. Clearly he'd finished his phone call, because he sprang to his feet and came around the desk with hand outstretched. "Owen! Great to see you." Firm shake, and a clap on the back.

Although they were both close to six feet tall, no one would take them for brothers, Owen mused as he returned the greeting. At forty-five, Boone had deeply tanned skin and nearly black hair with a sprinkling of silver like his father, whom Owen had met a few times long ago. By contrast, Owen's russet hair, untouched by gray at thirty-seven, reflected their mother's Irish heritage, while his light complexion hinted at his father's Russian background. "Sorry to interrupt. You did get my text about picking up the key, right?"

"No problem." From a drawer, Boone fished a house key. "Right here."

"But that's…" Phyllis hesitated.

"What?" Her husband shot her a puzzled look.

"You know I…"

The phone rang. "Got to take this," Boone said without checking the display. "Glad you're here, Owen. I'm proud of my famous kid bro."

"Not as famous as I plan to be," Owen shot back.

A grin, a half wave, and Boone was lost in his phone conversation.

Frowning, Phyllis retreated into the hall. "Have you had lunch? I could scare up a sandwich out of the fridge."

"No, thanks. I'll grab something at the hospital." He needed to get back. Even a half-hour break was longer than he usually allowed himself. Although he'd been coordinating the fertility program long-distance from Boston, the most intense preparations for the official opening remained, and he'd spent a good part of the morning in the O.R. On arrival, he'd found a waiting list of eager patients and, while scheduling operations in addition to his administrative duties made for fourteen-hour days, performing surgery energized Owen.

"I should…" Phyllis cleared her throat. "Have you met my little sister?"

He hadn't known she had one. "Afraid not." Usually, families got together at weddings, but when Phyllis and Boone eloped to Las Vegas, Owen had learned about it by phone.

"As a matter of fact, Bailey's a nurse at the hospital," she said. "She's twelve years younger than me, so I was kind of her second mother."

Owen didn't pay much attention to nurses unless they assisted him directly. "Which doctor does she work with?"

"Nora Kendall. Oh, wait, she got married. It's Nora Franco now."

Ah, Nora Franco—one of the thorns in Owen's side. The ob-gyn made no secret of the fact that she disagreed with Owen's policy of moving full speed ahead with fertility patients. Instead of steering them into assisted reproductive technologies such as in vitro fertilization as quickly as possible, Nora preferred to try old-fashioned approaches, one at a time, month after month.

Not only did that lower the hospital's conception rate, but it discouraged patients. Recently, two of Nora's patients had stopped their treatments to adopt babies. Owen preferred to help couples give birth to their own genetic offspring if that was what they wanted, and he expected cooperation from all the Safe Harbor ob-gyns, including those like Nora, for whom fertility issues composed only a part of their caseload. "I know Dr. Franco. We have a few things to work out."

"Well, Bailey's crazy about her," Phyllis said.

"As she should be." Doctors counted on their nurses' loyalty. "Listen, I'd love to stay and chat, but I'm interrupting your work, and I've got a long afternoon and evening ahead. Let's schedule some time together, the three of us."

"Oh. Sure. But—"

"I'll give you a call." Owen didn't want to snap at his sister-in-law, but her fluttery manner was beginning to irritate him.

As he went out to his car, he had to admit he was also annoyed that they'd hired a surrogate without bothering to tell him. Not that he'd have objected, but depending on the nature of Phyllis's medical problem, perhaps she could have been helped to conceive on her own.

Until today, Owen had scarcely given a second thought to the fact that he was going to be a father. So why did he find himself wishing he'd asked Phyllis whether they'd used her own eggs or the surrogate's?

Either way, a stranger was having his baby. Well, so what? Inseminations with donated sperm were old tech, and the use of surrogates dated back to the Bible.

At the new laboratories being set up at Safe Harbor, all sorts of conceptions would be possible. He'd donated genetic material, that's all. Men did it every day, Owen told himself as he started the engine. What was done, was done.

Putting the car in gear, he headed back to work.

You COULD NEVER TELL about Friday afternoons, Bailey reflected as she plopped into a chair at the nurses' station, adjusted the expandable maternity waistband on her pink uniform and slid the shoes off her swollen feet. All too often, patients ignored their symptoms until they realized the weekend was at hand, and then showed up en masse without appointments.

Other days, like this one, patients cancelled appointments and nobody else stopped in. She supposed you could blame Southern Californians' love of going on vacation. You'd think people who lived amid palm trees and ocean breezes would stay put, but they didn't.

At four-thirty, Nora had instructed everyone to go home early. "Especially you," she'd told Bailey.

"I just need to clean up a few details," Bailey had protested. And here she was, half an hour later, with the office in apple-pie order. She hated to see her doctor arrive on Monday morning and find that the cleaning crew had missed some old coffee cups or that they'd run out of exam gloves in the right size.

Also, she wanted to take her blood pressure and check her baby's heart rate with the Doppler stethoscope. And she could only do that when no one was around.

She'd be horribly embarrassed to admit to Nora that she'd lied about having had her three-month checkup in L.A. last Saturday. The truth was, Phyllis and Boone hadn't paid the doctor due to a cash-flow problem and, while Bailey had fronted the money the first two months, her bank account was running low. These days, each paycheck was spent almost before she cashed it.

If only they hadn't insisted on using the L.A. clinic, which didn't accept Bailey's insurance. But Phyllis had felt they'd be risking their privacy by arranging the surrogacy at Safe Harbor. Bailey supposed that was a reasonable point, and she wanted Phyllis to be happy.

That's why she'd been willing to bear a child for her older sister, who'd essentially raised her while their irresponsible mom flitted from one man to another. It was a privilege to carry Phyllis and Boone's baby. And it *was* their baby, in every meaningful sense. Since Bailey figured she shared at least half her genes with her sister, that meant this little guy or girl was three-quarters the same as if they'd been able to have a baby on their own.

Still, Bailey couldn't help worrying. She was big for three months; most people assumed she was about five months along, like Nora, who was due in November. Bailey assured everyone she was fine, quoting her doctor in L.A. The one she hadn't seen for a month.

What if there's more than one baby?

That would be a blessing for Phyllis and Boone. But it meant Bailey's prenatal care and delivery would become even more complicated, and who was going to pay for that?

Well, she'd better get moving while she had the office to herself. If she stuck around too long, one of the nurses from an adjacent office might notice her late departure and wonder what she was up to. Gossip ran rampant at Safe Harbor, and Bailey was already too much of a target, thanks to her surrogacy.

As she eased onto her feet, leaving off the shoes that pinched like crazy, she heard the waiting room door open. Patients often got confused in the large medical office building and mistook it for the hospital next door. Dredging up a pleasant expression, she padded out. "Can I help you?"

An impatient glare swept over her, and then the lean, tightly wound man in the white coat returned his attention to some papers on his clipboard. After all the publicity about the new head of the fertility program, every employee at Safe Harbor instantly recognized Dr. Owen Tartikoff, and dreaded his infamously acid tongue.

While the man got along well with his surgical nurse, who'd moved here from Boston to join him, he'd already chased off his first office nurse and reportedly was having trouble with his second. What was he doing in Nora's office at five o'clock on a Friday? And how much fuss was he going to make because the doctor wasn't around to respond to yet another of his directives from on high?

Technically, he wasn't Nora's boss—that would be the hospital administrator, Dr. Mark Rayburn—but Dr. T. appeared to believe he ran every aspect of Safe Harbor that touched on fertility treatments. And since he was the darling of the corporation that owned the hospital, Dr. Rayburn allowed him a lot of leeway.

The man still hadn't bothered to speak, so Bailey took the initiative. "Dr. Franco's left for the day." *Now go away and leave me to my checkup.*

He took his time jotting a note. Didn't the man care that she was standing here awaiting his response?

"Well?" Bailey demanded. "Can I do something for you or not?"

That got his attention. Startled, cinnamon-colored eyes flared at her and then burned a trail down her enlarged body, from her shoulder-length, curly brown hair all the way to her feet. "Where are your shoes?"

She resisted the urge to curl her toes like a kid. "I took them off." *Can't you see I'm pregnant?*

He could, obviously, because he was taking another assessing look at her midsection. "You're the nurse?"

"Bailey Wayne," she confirmed.

"Nurse practitioner?"

"Not yet." Although she'd earned her degree as a registered nurse, she hadn't qualified to provide routine care for her own patients. Once she delivered the baby, she planned to take additional courses, paying with returns from the savings she'd invested with Phyllis and Boone.

The doctor tapped his pen against the clipboard. "When will Dr. Franco be back?"

"On Monday," Bailey said.

"When is she on call?" The obstetricians took turns being available to deliver babies.

"Tomorrow morning," Bailey said. "Why?"

He regarded her coldly. "We need to discuss some of her cases."

The notion offended Bailey. "Why are you reviewing her cases?"

"Do you object?" Dr. T. stared down at her from what appeared to be a towering height.

Being only five foot four on a good day, Bailey felt at an additional disadvantage without her shoes. "Well, there's the issue of patient privacy," she said.

"Overseeing the quality of fertility care is my responsibility," he snapped.

As if it weren't Nora's! But she could see in his grim expression that she'd overstepped her bounds. *Bite your tongue.* "Yes, Doctor."

He was studying her abdomen again. What exactly did he expect to learn through her uniform? she wondered. For once, she appreciated her sister's discretion in seeking out a clinic elsewhere. No way would she want this arrogant doctor prowling through her medical records.

"You're Phyllis's sister," he said abruptly.

That startled her. "How do you know Phyllis?"

A pucker formed between his eyebrows. "She didn't tell you about my relationship to Boone?"

He must be one of their investors. "She doesn't discuss business with me."

Mercifully, a light tap at the open door cut off further discussion. Hospital public relations director Jennifer Martin peered inside. "Oh, there you are! Dr. Tartikoff, the TV news crew is here. Remember, they called earlier, wanting comments on the septuplets born in Newport Beach?"

"Right." With a subtle straightening of the shoulders and relaxing of the jaw, he transformed from a nosy know-it-all to a gracious, self-possessed expert. "I'd be happy to answer their questions, as long as they understand that I'm speaking in general terms."

"They're aware that you have no involvement in the case." Jennifer, a pretty dark-haired woman, seemed in awe of the distinguished surgeon. She stepped back, holding the door for him.

Bailey supposed Dr. T. was used to being consulted by the press. Since the doctors directly involved in famous fertility cases couldn't speak about them without their clients' permission, reporters often sought outside experts for insight and news bites. No doubt Jennifer encouraged them, since the publicity would benefit Safe Harbor's fertility program.

Just when Bailey thought she was safely rid of him, Dr. T. paused in the doorway and skewered her with a frown. "Miss Wayne, is it your custom to hang around the office barefoot when everyone else has left?"

"I was on my way out."

"We'll wait."

Much as she'd have liked to tell him to butt out, she didn't want to make him or Jennifer suspicious. A doctor's office contained restricted medications, and even the slightest hint that she might be abusing her position could seriously harm her *and* Nora. Yielding to the inevitable, Bailey fetched her shoes and purse, and locked the door behind her.

Once they exited the building, the PR director hustled Dr. T. toward the adjacent hospital. His tall straight body swung along the walkway with a powerful gait, the white coat emphasizing his broad shoulders.

Full of himself, of course. Bailey never dated doctors because most of them had a God complex, and here was a perfect example.

Not that she'd had great experiences with any of the

other men who'd wandered through her life, either, including the one she'd married and divorced when she was still in college. Maybe someday she'd find true love, but in the meantime she had more pressing matters to deal with.

Like needing a checkup.

Although she was tempted to sneak back into the medical center, other offices were now closing and she risked being seen. The money situation was intolerable. She had to talk to Phyllis about it, but that could wait. Tonight, she just wanted to crash, not to mention put her feet up.

A few minutes later, with a sense of relief, Bailey steered her battle-scarred compact car inland along Safe Harbor Boulevard. She drove through a modest middle-class neighborhood to Morningstar Circle, where, sheltered in a thick cluster of squatty palms and ferns, lay the beach-style house that was her refuge.

To compensate for asking her to front the money for medical bills, Phyllis had given her a key when the renter moved out last month, and Bailey loved everything about the place, from the tropical ambiance to the open design of the rooms. Here, amid lush greenery, she could relax in the whirlpool bath and enjoy her weekend in blissful solitude.

Chapter Two

The TV crew had set up in Owen's office on the hospital's fifth floor. When he entered with Jennifer, a fortyish man in a sport jacket shook his hand and introduced himself in a deep and important tone as Hayden O'Donnell. Obviously, he expected everyone to recognize him, and Owen did his best to play along.

Cooperating with the media was important. While some physicians hated this intrusion into their real work, publicity played a vital role in securing funding for technology and research.

With a wall of medical certificates as a backdrop, Owen assumed a pleasant expression and framed his answers to avoid seeming unduly critical of the doctors who'd handled this particular case. Ethical guidelines called for limiting the number of embryos implanted, and septuplets presented a risk to mother and babies, he explained. However, the patients were doing well, and that was what mattered most.

As soon as he could, he steered the subject to his program's grand opening in September and the state-of-the-art facilities they were installing.

"Weren't you originally supposed to have a separate facility dedicated to your program?" asked O'Donnell.

Either he was better informed than most reporters or Jennifer had briefed him in advance.

"It was our plan to convert a nearby dental building, but the owner went into bankruptcy and matters got tied up in court," Owen said. "Rather than delay, we're fitting our facilities into the existing hospital. It's a challenge, but my staff is rising to it."

A few questions later, the reporter thanked him and signed off. "Great interview," Jennifer commented after the crew had gone. "They'll be running clips all evening."

"Thanks for your help." Although he had a well-deserved reputation for riding roughshod over underlings, Owen tried to limit his caustic comments to those who deserved them. Jennifer Martin was good at her job.

Soon she departed. Wondering how to make the best use of his time, he checked his watch. Friday, 6:00 p.m.

The other office in the suite was dark. Alec Denny, Ph.D, director of laboratories, had left for the weekend. Owen couldn't fault his associate, who'd moved from Boston several months in advance to transform the hospital basement into labs equipped to handle all aspects of assisted fertilization. Alec, divorced with a five-year-old daughter, had wasted no time renewing old acquaintances. The Safe Harbor native had recently become engaged to his high school sweetheart.

That was how most men created families, by finding the right woman and marrying her. Owen, however, took little interest in children once they passed the embryo stage. *I'm not the daddy type,* he'd told more than one girlfriend over the years.

Even donating sperm at his brother's request had made barely a blip on his mental radar. His only concern, as he'd commented to Boone, was that the kid might inherit his very different coloring, but his brother had assured him that everyone would assume it came from Phyllis, who had also been a redhead once upon a time.

When he'd learned of the pregnancy, however, Owen had been surprised at how fascinated he became. He'd begun sneaking glances at young children, wondering how it would feel to see one who was descended from him.

Learning about the surrogate today made him uneasy. True, once the baby was born, he assumed it would grow up safe and happy with his brother and sister-in-law, leaving Owen to play the doting but distant uncle. Still, he didn't like the way Boone and Phyllis had thrown him a curve ball. Not only was there this business of a surrogate, but what about Phyllis's pregnant sister?

For all he knew, Bailey might be married and expecting a child with her husband, though she hadn't been wearing a ring. On the other hand, she might have removed it because of swelling.

Was *she* the surrogate? Her bulge was large for three months of gestation, but every woman carried a pregnancy differently, and Bailey was short. Cute, too, if you went for that type, which Owen usually didn't. Tall, elegant women were more his style. He preferred his girlfriends cool, remote and safe. He'd only come close to losing his heart once, a long time ago, to a fellow medical resident. Luckily, she'd been just as ambitious as he was, and they'd parted by mutual consent.

Phyllis might be using a clinic in L.A., yet here was Bailey right under his nose. He wished now that he hadn't been in such a hurry to leave his brother's house this afternoon. No wonder Phyllis had hemmed and hawed. Maybe she'd been trying to raise a touchy subject.

Was her cheeky sister carrying his child?

As Owen leaned back, he kept seeing that defiant face with its sprinkling of freckles and flashing green eyes.

Usually, he refused to tolerate insubordination, but he had to admire the nurse's loyalty to her doctor. The way she'd stood up to him had taken courage, and a touch of fool-hardiness, as well.

Was she reckless? That might explain her decision to carry her sister's baby, if that's what she was doing. And given her open manner, he had no doubt she'd told everyone within earshot the whole story. But surely she was ignorant of Owen's involvement. Judging by her reaction to his mention of Boone, she hadn't had a clue they were related.

A chill crept over him. The last thing he would tolerate was being the subject of hospital gossip about something as personal as donating sperm to his brother. If Bailey *was* carrying his baby, he had to do his best to stop others from hearing about it, including her.

Eventually, she'd learn that he and Boone were siblings, but since his brother and sister-in-law clearly valued their privacy as much as he did, the details of this conception should remain a secret.

It was better to quit wasting time on personal speculation. At his computer, Owen clicked to a folder of applications for surgical fellowships. For three funded positions, he'd received dozens of résumés, including a number from other countries. Not only did he intend to pick the best-qualified and most interesting candidates, he had to consider their areas of expertise to ensure the best possible balance.

Fifteen minutes later, he'd scanned half a dozen applications without remembering a word of what he'd read. Owen closed the folder and logged off. Dinner at the cafeteria should jumpstart his concentration.

He was on his way downstairs when his cell rang. Concerned

that one of the morning's surgical patients had suffered a complication, he answered fast. "Dr. Tartikoff."

"This is Long and Short Movers," said a male voice with a Boston accent. "Double-checking the address you gave us. That's 587 Morningstar Circle, Safe Harbor, California, right, Doc?"

"Yes, but I wasn't expecting you till Monday." He'd planned to go through the house and figure out a layout for the furniture.

"Well, we're here," the man said. "Problem is, there's some woman, a Miss Wayne, claiming we're at the wrong house. She says she lives here."

For a moment, Owen couldn't breathe.

So that's what Phyllis had been trying to tell him. Not about Bailey being the surrogate but that she lived in the house.

Or, possibly, both.

"So what do you want us to do?" the mover prompted.

Owen resisted the urge to bang his forehead on the nearest wall. *I want you to go away and return in another reality where the secret mother of my child isn't living in my house.*

"Hang on," he said. "I'll be right there."

So much for a peaceful, productive evening. He had to get this matter straightened out fast.

BAILEY COULDN'T HAVE heard right. The moving man said he'd just put in a call to—

"Dr. *Owen* Tartikoff?" she repeated.

"You know the guy?" The solidly built fellow stood with arms folded as they both regarded the van blocking the end of Morningstar Circle.

"Yes, but I have no idea why he's trying to move into my house." Surely Phyllis and Boone hadn't rented the place out from under her. But then, Bailey had to admit, she could never tell what they might do.

It didn't help her mood that she was starving, or that delicious aromas were wafting from the far side of a cinderblock wall that ran along one edge of the property. Beyond it lay the Suncrest supermarket and Waffle Heaven, which cooked up great brunches and dinners.

"Nice place. Great landscaping." The guy indicated the array of fan palms, birds of paradise and hibiscus.

"Yes. It's cool." The low, open house reminded Bailey of a tiki room set in a rain forest. She loved this restful oasis, even if the rumble of delivery vans did shatter the morning calm at a ridiculously early hour.

It wasn't the type of house she imagined Owen Tartikoff living in. No doubt he'd prefer someplace formal and stuffy, with perfectly clipped hedges instead of lush greenery and abundant flowers. If she raised enough of a fuss, no doubt he'd find some other, more suitable quarters. Anyway, she refused to give up her refuge.

The mover and his assistant sat on the front planter and unwrapped sandwiches. Bailey phoned Phyllis. She hadn't gotten out more than a few words when her sister said, "I'm sorry."

"How long have you known that Dr. Tartikoff was moving in?" Bailey swatted her neck and discovered that what she'd assumed was a pesky mosquito was in fact a tendril of bougainvillea. The shrubbery was overdue for pruning.

"Since Boone sprang it on me this afternoon. I wanted to call you but we got tied up with clients." Phyllis coughed apologetically, or at least, Bailey hoped her sister felt apologetic, and not just guilty at telling a big fat lie.

"Well?" she demanded. "What are you going to do about it?"

"There's not much we can do," Phyllis said. "He co-owns the house."

"What?" These past few months, Bailey had heard plenty about Dr. Owen Tartikoff's background, but all of the information focused on New York and Boston. No mention of any connection to Safe Harbor. "How did that happen?"

"He and Boone are half brothers."

Bailey's knees threatened to give out. She plopped onto a low bench surrounded by daylilies. "I never knew Boone had a brother."

"I was planning to invite you both to dinner and introduce you."

So that's what Dr. T. had meant about his relationship to Boone. Funny that no one else at the hospital seemed aware of the fact, but then, neither man was advertising it. "Don't they get along?"

"Oh, they get along fine," Phyllis said.

"He did know I'm your sister," Bailey conceded. "He mentioned it this afternoon."

"You don't actually work together, do you?"

Now, why should Phyllis care about that? "No. He stopped by to see Nora. But he didn't say anything about moving in with me."

"I tried to explain about your living situation when he picked up the key, but he ran off too fast."

How unthinkable, for the high and mighty head of the fertility program to share quarters with a lowly nurse. Especially one who sided with her doctor against him when they disagreed on treatment plans.

What was she going to do? Bailey had already given up the apartment she'd shared with a couple of friends, and she couldn't afford to rent a place on her own. "I'll have to come live with you until the baby's born."

Her sister responded with a strangled squawk. Hardly encouraging.

"You're leasing that huge place," Bailey pointed out. "Lots of empty rooms." Filled with rented furniture, but empty of humans.

"Boone would never allow it." Phyllis sounded breathless. "Bailey, you have no idea the pressure we're under. Why can't you both stay there? The house has three bedrooms."

"Two," Bailey said grimly. "And they share a bathroom."

"We lived in places smaller than that when we were growing up," her sister reminded her.

"Yes, but we were a family."

"Good news! You and Owen are related by marriage, so that makes you family, too. I have to go. You'll work this out. I have faith!" With a click, Phyllis was gone.

She and Owen were family? Bailey couldn't decide whether to laugh or cry.

No time to worry about that, because here came a black Lexus with Dr. T. at the wheel. Since the van was obstructing the driveway, he stopped a few doors down, got out and strode toward her, shading his eyes against the low-lying, but still powerful, evening sun. "I didn't expect to see you again today."

Bailey dragged herself upright. "The feeling's mutual."

"I'm sure you've spoken to your sister by now," the doctor went on. "And she's explained that I own this place."

"Half own," Bailey corrected. "I'm living in the other half."

"I don't recall it being a duplex."

"It isn't."

She had the sense that they were squaring off to do battle. Her opponent was considerably taller than her and a lot more domineering. On the other hand, Bailey figured that, with the baby, she counted as two, so she had him outnumbered.

The movers watched silently but with a great deal of interest. Bailey wondered if they were taking bets and, if so, who they were backing.

"Do you have a lot of furniture?" Dr. T. asked.

"What does that have to do with anything?"

"Just answer the question."

"Do cushions and a futon count?" Her apartment had been crammed with her roommates' furnishings, so she'd never acquired much.

He gestured at the enormous van. "I have an entire houseful inherited from my parents. Putting it into storage would be a fortune, on top of the cost of moving it again."

"So we're deciding this on the basis of who's going to suffer the most financially?" Bailey didn't see why he got to set the terms. "I have a better idea. Let's do rock, paper, scissors."

Disbelief flashed across his high-boned face, and then he started to laugh. Amazingly, the man looked almost human. Not only human, but kind of sweet.

Must be a hallucination fueled by hunger pangs. "Well?" Bailey demanded.

He cleared his throat. "I've got a key and I'm moving in. Will I be able to tell which bedroom is yours?"

"The smaller one. I've been using the master bedroom as a study."

"The master bedroom will suit me fine."

"But we can't possibly live together!" The idea was just weird.

He blew out a long breath. "I've got too much on my plate these next few weeks to mess with finding a house, especially when I happen to own this one. I suppose the fact that we're sort of related might make our living together slightly less scandalous."

"In Southern California, this doesn't even come close to scandalous. But…"

He strode past her, signaling to the movers. "You fellows get started unloading while I take a look around."

"Right you are, Doc," said the larger of the pair. As he passed Bailey, he gave her a sympathetic wink.

She balled her fists in protest, but what could she do? Since it went against her nature to do nothing, she looked through the numbers in her cell phone. Her friend Patty was a former police officer turned detective. Perfect! If there was a legal loophole, she'd find it.

Bailey placed the call. "So, hey," came her friend's reassuring voice. "What's up with Little Mommy?"

Bailey explained, which took some doing. Fortunately, Patty, who'd known Bailey since high school, wasn't easily shocked. "I wondered about that deal with your sister, letting you move into the house instead of paying your medical bills. You have to admit, it's unusual."

"None of which solves the immediate problem. I mean, can you imagine me living with Dr. Tartikoff? Everybody hates him."

"Everybody being Nora," her friend corrected. "Alec likes him fine."

Patty's fiancé was Owen's close associate. "Alec's more or less his equal. That's different."

"In your condition, there could be advantages to having an ob-gyn on the premises," Patty noted.

That would be true if he weren't the last man on earth Bailey wanted snooping into her situation. "Seriously, can't you think of some legal justification to throw him out? Like invasion of privacy?"

"Sorry, no. But remember the old saying—keep your friends close and your enemies closer."

"I never thought that included sharing a bathroom," Bailey grumbled.

"Don't you live right behind a supermarket that has early morning deliveries?" Patty asked.

"Yes."

"He won't last long."

"You don't know doctors." Bailey sighed. "They can sleep through anything. If not, they'd never survive their residency. Thanks anyway."

"Keep me posted," Patty said.

As she tucked away the phone, Bailey dodged back to avoid getting bowled over by a formal sofa that, in her opinion, would be right at home in a funeral parlor. The movers toted it up the walkway toward the double doors, which Owen had flung wide.

His mouth twisted as he regarded Bailey. It was the smirk of a man who enjoyed winning.

Well, let him enjoy his moment of triumph. At the hospital, he might be the great Dr. Tartikoff, but he'd just moved in with a woman who wouldn't hesitate to take his ego down a notch.

She was almost looking forward to it.

Chapter Three

Owen didn't recall the house having such an open design, but then, on his only previous visit while attending a medical conference in L.A., he'd rushed through to approve Boone's choice of an investment. He certainly hadn't been thinking in terms of living here himself.

In the low-ceilinged living room, his parents' antique furniture looked painfully out of place, hunkering heavily around a plant-filled atrium. Bamboo wallpaper lined the master bedroom, which opened on to the patio and spa through a sliding glass door that appeared to be the only rear exit from the house. Then there was a single bathroom, which connected the bedrooms.

By the time the movers left, it was after eight o'clock and boxes filled every available space. A couple of large table lamps remained swathed in packing materials. Wishing he hadn't moved a cartoon-character pole lamp into Bailey's bedroom, Owen stumbled through near-darkness into the dimly lit kitchen.

Seeing a small, glum figure eating yogurt at the breakfast table, Owen felt an unaccustomed twinge of guilt. True, her furniture in the main rooms had consisted mainly of flowered cushions and a card table, all of which fit into her bedroom, but he'd been ruthless about taking over the house. He supposed he could at least have asked her opinion about where to place his entertainment center.

Too hungry to frame an apology and too impatient to wait for a pizza, he peered into the fridge. "I don't suppose you have one of those you can spare?"

"You like yogurt?"

"I'll eat it when I'm starving." He didn't see any, though.

"This was the last one. I'm also out of raw red meat you can rip off the bone."

How did she know he preferred a good steak? "This will do." He took out a block of cheese and some bread, fixed open-face slices and popped them in her toaster oven. "Look, I don't plan to be here much except to eat breakfast and sleep."

"That's good news." She moved her legs away quickly as he sat down, as if any contact between them might burn.

Owen could carry his food into the other room, but he didn't feel like it. In fact, he rather enjoyed having this freckle-faced young woman keep him company. In the silence of the house, he felt for the first time exactly how far away he'd moved from everyone and everything familiar.

In the Boston area, where he'd lived and worked since arriving at Harvard Medical School, he'd had a favorite café—in Cambridge actually. All he had to do was take a table and soon he'd be joined by friends and colleagues, people as passionate as he was about discussing the latest world news and medical developments.

The funny thing was that, right now, Owen couldn't picture anyone in particular. He missed the environment, not the individuals. As for the food, melted cheese on toast tasted remarkably good, he discovered as he began to eat.

After polishing off the meal, he addressed his companion. "We should lay down a few ground rules."

"I take my morning shower at seven-thirty," she announced. "You'll have to work around that."

He didn't like being ordered about. "It's not up to you to dictate terms."

She propped her elbows on the table. "Let's get one thing straight. At work, you may be Dr. Tartikoff and you may be way higher on the food chain. At home, you're the guy who moved into my house and stole my cheese."

"I plan to replace it. The bread, too." He made a mental note to find a supermarket tomorrow and buy a supply of frozen dinners, as well.

That remark disappeared into the pool of her disapproval without a ripple. "And as you may have noticed, the only rear exit is through your room, so when I want to use the spa, I will knock once, wait five seconds, and then walk through. With my eyes closed, sort of."

"Sort of?"

"You've got this place so crammed with junk, I'll have bruises all over my shins if I'm not careful." Even in the faint light from the ceiling globe, her green eyes managed to flash fire.

Owen enjoyed teasing her, but this raised a serious subject. "You shouldn't be using the spa. Water that hot isn't healthy for pregnant women or their babies."

"I lowered the temperature," she told him. "Anything else you think an obstetrical nurse is too stupid to know?"

Didn't she understand that he'd only meant to protect her? Well, if she was determined to take offense, he might as well continue. "Since you're a professional, I hope you realize how awkward it could be if our living arrangement became common gossip."

"Oh?"

"For example…I don't suppose you could avoid mentioning it to Dr. Franco?"

Bailey shook her head, sending curls tumbling across her forehead. Owen felt an inexplicable temptation to brush back those rebellious strands. "I don't keep secrets from Nora."

He'd assumed as much. "All right. But I'd appreciate your not mentioning this to anyone else."

"Well…" She bit her lip.

Now that he thought about it, he'd seen her on the phone while the movers were working. "Who else did you call?"

"Just my friend Patty."

"Does she work at the hospital?"

"No."

He felt a rush of relief. "Good."

"I'm sure her fiancé won't tell anyone," Bailey went on.

"He works there?" It seemed as if everybody in this town was linked to each other. "And her fiancé is….?"

"Alec."

"Is that supposed to mean something…Alec *Denny?*" He saw the answer in her rueful expression. "Oh, wonderful." His closest associate was marrying this woman's best friend. If Owen had nurtured even the slightest hope that secrets might be kept, this smashed it to rubble.

Much as he itched to ask about her pregnancy, he'd better steer clear of that subject. Because if he weren't careful, Bailey Wayne would find out the whole story about her baby's paternity. And so would the entire town of Safe Harbor.

If a juicy item like this reached the press, Owen could imagine the jokes on late-night talk shows. *Did you hear about the fertility doctor who took his job a little too seriously?* The backlash would tarnish his entire program.

"You could move out," Bailey said sweetly.

Owen gritted his teeth. If he possessed a magic wand, he'd gladly have removed his possessions, but he simply didn't have time to deal with this. "I'm performing surgery in the morning." Another thought struck him. "And I still have to find my sheets and towels for tonight."

His roommate tossed her empty yogurt carton into the wastebasket. "Have fun."

Owen cleared his tableware and began fitting everything inside the dishwasher. "Since it's the weekend, I presume you sleep late. I set my alarm for 6:00 a.m. I'll try to be quiet in the bathroom."

"Oh, you'll be awake before that," Bailey said.

He shot her what he hoped was a quelling glance. "I expect you to be considerate."

"I'm not the problem." With a beatific smile and no further comment, she sauntered out of the kitchen. A moment later, he heard the click of her bedroom door.

They must have early rising neighbors, or possibly barking dogs nearby, although he hadn't heard any so far. Surely no one in this neighborhood kept a rooster. He hadn't moved to Outer Farmovia, had he?

Dismissing the matter, he went to unpack his sheets.

OWEN AWOKE IN A SHIFTING darkness pierced by what seemed to be headlights playing through the vertical blinds in his bedroom. Groping on the bedside table, he found that his cell phone read 3:25 a.m.

What was that rumbling noise? He must have been hearing it in his sleep. His dreams, when he remembered them at all, usually involved replaying surgeries and reviewing patient charts, but now he recalled huddling behind a barbed-wire fence while military-style trucks rolled past. The frightening scene seemed ripped from an old film about a Soviet prisoner-of-war camp.

From outside came the squeal of hydraulic brakes, followed by silence. He sat up, struggling to shake off his disorientation. He hadn't been recalling a film but vivid images he'd formed as a teenager after reading articles his father had written for a Russian émigré newspaper about his own imprisonment. Although weakened by years of incarceration as a dissident, Yevgeny Tartikoff had survived and moved to America, where he'd eked out a living as a writer and editor. He'd been pleased by his son's interest in medicine, but had died while Owen was still an undergraduate.

More rumbling set Owen's heart pounding. Those were real trucks, and real lights glaring through the blinds....

Oh, you'll be awake before that. This must be what Bailey had meant. He'd noticed a high wall behind the property, but the tangle of vegetation had blocked whatever lay on the other side. A business that received early morning deliveries, obviously.

Despite his annoyance, Owen had to smile. Bailey must have enjoyed her little joke. Right now she was probably sleeping soundly thanks to a good set of earplugs, dreaming about her unwanted roommate departing posthaste with his furniture in tow.

Well, she was about to learn that Owen Tartikoff was no lightweight. In his phone's organizer, he added earplugs to his shopping list, then scooted down on the bed and pulled the pillow over his head.

Doing his best to ignore the rattle and bang of trucks pulling up to a loading dock, he drifted off.

"YOU LIVE BEHIND A SUPERMARKET?" Nurse Erica Benford chuckled as she watched Owen. He appreciated the way she stood ready to anticipate his needs as he performed a hysteroscopy on an anesthetized thirty-seven-year-old woman who'd been trying for years to have a second child. The minimally invasive surgery involved inserting a thin scope equipped with a camera that allowed him to remove small fibroids and adhesions. There was a good chance he could clean out the obstacles to conception, and since the procedure avoided the need for an incision, recovery should be swift.

"I drove by the Suncrest Market on my way here," he said as he worked. "Big place with a pharmacy, deli, the whole shot. And how's this for irony? There was a sign in the window advertising sleep aids."

"You don't suppose Bailey paid someone to put that up for your benefit, do you?" Erica teased.

"I wouldn't put it past her. Maybe I should move out, but I take this situation as a challenge." Owen had filled Erica in about his living arrangements, since she already knew he planned to occupy a house he co-owned. Also, he preferred to let her spread the word quietly before Bailey got a chance to put a colorful spin on things.

"So Dr. Franco's nurse is your sister-in-law's sister. Now, there's an interesting twist. I haven't met her yet, but I'm sure I will." Small, blonde and dedicated, Erica hadn't originally planned to move to California. Then she'd announced that her troubled marriage had broken up and she was eager for a fresh start. Lucky for Owen.

He stayed alert to the other people around them, especially the anesthesiologist, Dr. Rod Vintner, who kept a close watch on the patient's heart rate, blood pressure and other vital signs. Having a state-of-the-art surgical suite meant a lot, of course. Not only did the surgeon get to manipulate the coolest tools in the medical field, but an overhead camera recorded each operation for later review, while an adjacent pathology lab permitted immediate examination of tissue, and computer terminals allowed him to review test results without leaving the sterile environment. Still, there was no substitute for skilled, reliable personnel.

"You *are* aware that Bailey's pregnant with her sister's child, right?" It was the first time Rod had joined the conversation, but clearly he'd been listening. To them, *and* to hospital chitchat.

Silently, Owen thanked him for confirming the fact of Bailey's surrogacy, even as he felt a spark of annoyance at having to learn about it from a man he hardly knew. "It should be interesting to watch my niece or nephew develop day by day."

"Do you have kids?" Rod asked.

Why was the fellow so nosy? But perhaps it seemed like a routine question to him.

Erica spared Owen the bother of answering. "Neither of us does. That's our joke, considering the kind of work we do. Personally, I prefer keeping my personal life neat and orderly."

"You have kids, Rod?" Owen was glad to steer the conversation away from himself.

"I thought I did." The anesthesiologist left that cryptic remark hanging in the air while he adjusted the patient's breathing tube. "When my ex-wife got ready to remarry, she produced DNA tests to prove our daughters weren't really mine. She tried to cut me off from seeing them, but the judge said they're still legally my responsibility. Big of him, wasn't it?" His voice caught. "All those years, I had no idea she'd cheated on me. I still feel like they're my girls."

What a heartbreaking mess. While Erica expressed sympathy, Owen kept his gaze on the patient. Best not to get involved, especially since his thoughts shifted defiantly to his own circumstances.

How often would he get to visit *his* baby? Although he was currently living near Boone and Phyllis, he had no rights at all, either as an uncle *or* a sperm donor. He supposed he should have considered that before he agreed to donate, but somehow it hadn't mattered until he learned about the surrogacy. And until he met Bailey.

This morning, she'd padded into the kitchen wearing a Cheshire-cat grin and asked how he'd slept. "Fine," he'd answered truthfully, since he did feel energetic despite his restless night. He'd also appreciated the way the morning light bathed Bailey in gentle radiance, as if she were a fertility goddess.

A what? Owen nearly choked at the ridiculous image. It probably stemmed from living in a tropical rain forest.

The conversation continued around him, with Erica sharing horror stories about *her* ex, who'd dumped her for a rich woman who would support him in style. Anyone listening to this conversation would vow never to marry. A better conclusion, in Owen's opinion, would be to choose one's spouse very, very carefully.

If he had a list of qualifications, it included an advanced degree and a distinguished career. Also the kind of sophistication that inspired maître d's to guide the woman to the best table in the house.

There was no place on that list for an impish smile and a refusal to be intimidated by a famous surgeon invading her refrigerator. Or for a nature generous enough to bear a child for her sister.

Maybe there should be. But he drew the line at a woman who hogged the bathroom counter with a ridiculous array of creams and ointments, and who'd dumped his toiletries into a drawer without even asking. He hadn't bothered to fight that battle...yet.

Focusing his attention on the procedure, he made a final assessment to ensure he'd done a thorough job. Satisfied, Owen retracted the scope, thanked his staff and went to talk to the patient's husband.

He found the man pacing in the waiting room. "Everything looks great," Owen said. "She's doing fine."

"When can I see her?" he asked.

"In about an hour." Owen explained that the man's wife was on her way to the recovery room and that he could join her once she returned to her bed in the Same-Day Surgery Unit.

"Thanks, Doc." The man pumped his hand gratefully. "I'm willing to adopt, but she's set on having a second baby. I just want her to be happy. She's the reason I get up in the morning. As long as she's okay, that's all that matters."

"Of course."

Being able to enrich patients' lives was one of the most rewarding aspects of his job, Owen reflected. But in pursuing the goal of having a child, women ran risks, from taking hormones to going under anesthesia. Even for a healthy young woman, carrying a child could be hazardous. Just look at Bailey. Why *was* she so large?

That was, he reminded himself, between her and her doctor. And Phyllis and Boone, of course.

Owen went to prepare for his next procedure, a myomectomy to remove large uterine fibroids. He was reviewing the case on a monitor in an alcove when he heard a couple of staff members walk by.

Normally, he ignored the ever present hum of voices, but this time he couldn't. "They're sharing the same house?" the man was saying.

"I can't wait to hear what Bailey thinks about that!" the woman replied, and then coughed as she spotted Owen. Averting her face, she scurried on.

Well, great. The conversation in the operating room, which had no doubt been overheard by a number of people, had already become common gossip. While he'd known this was likely to happen, he hadn't expected word to spread this quickly, or for staffers to seize on it with such glee.

As long as they don't know you're the father, there's no reason for the press to get involved. Owen felt fairly certain about that. Still, who could tell what interested the local media? And since Bailey wasn't a patient at Safe Harbor, her coworkers weren't bound by the center's requirement of confidentiality. Just by common decency and discretion.

"You're kidding? He's the *uncle?*" boomed a male voice in the hallway, followed by shushing noises.

Owen felt the heat rise in his neck. In his younger years, friends used to enjoy embarrassing him just to watch the telltale flush. He'd mastered that response by focusing on being above such pettiness, and he resorted to the same attitude now.

"Is my next patient ready?" he snapped at the nearest nurse, the same blond fellow who'd just shot his mouth off about Owen being an uncle.

"I, uh, think she's been prepped," stammered the young man, whose name tag read Ned Norwalk, RN.

"I don't care what you think. I want to know if she's ready. Go find out."

Owen watched in satisfaction as the nurse hurried away with a subdued, "Yes, Doctor."

Owen was already beginning to regret letting the cat out of the bag today, but he'd only done so as a preemptive measure. That paled beside the stories Bailey was likely to spread. What if his every personal habit and dietary quirk became fodder for staff jokes?

Since he and Bailey were stuck with each other, they needed to have a serious discussion about respect. She might not be a patient at Safe Harbor, but she *was* an employee. And the reputation of the hospital and its new fertility program—not to mention Owen's personal privacy—trumped everything else.

He had a busy day ahead, but tonight he'd hash this out with her. This time, he didn't intend to let her one-up him, either.

Chapter Four

Bailey had given up long ago on understanding men. While there seemed to be some decent ones around, like her friends' husbands, in her experience you couldn't count on them. They disappeared when you needed them, like her father. Or they flaked out emotionally, like the young man she'd foolishly married at nineteen and divorced at twenty-one after she realized he was more interested in playing video games than in having a relationship.

The most puzzling man of all was Dr. Owen Tartikoff. She'd been hearing for months how abrasive he was, and she'd seen his arrogance for herself, yet this morning he'd grinned as if elated to see her scuffing into the kitchen in her oversize sleep shirt covered with anime figures. He hadn't groused about the trucks roaring into the supermarket lot last night. Amazingly, he hadn't even mentioned the fact that she'd dumped his shaver and cologne into a bathroom drawer, which she'd done specifically to annoy him.

Maybe he was on drugs. She didn't think so, though. A surgeon with a failing like that wouldn't last long.

Fortunately, he left early, giving her a chance to spend Saturday morning lounging around the house undisturbed, catching up on her internet contacts and taking a long nap.

After lunch, Bailey arrived at the Edward Serra Memorial Clinic for a shift as a volunteer peer counselor.

Housed in an annex next to the city's community center, the perpetually underfunded program had been established by pediatrician and activist Samantha Forrest as an alternative to traditional clinics. Here, pregnant teens, abused moms or anyone who needed a sympathetic ear and some guidance could wander in without worrying about appointments or paperwork.

The other volunteers included Nora, who was meeting with a young married couple this afternoon to discuss family planning, and Nora's husband, Leo, a police detective who sometimes counseled teen boys in need of a father figure, although he wasn't on-site today. As for Bailey, she didn't consider herself an expert on anything beyond nursing, but she was glad to serve as a caring friend.

While Nora used the counseling room, Bailey went outside to a picnic table with a woman who'd wandered over from an exercise class at the community center. Sitting across from her in the leafy shade, Renée Green had a strong rectangular face, light brown hair laced with gray, and tired eyes.

"I'm only sixty-two but I just don't have any purpose for living." Despite the July warmth, the woman folded her arms as if warding off a chill. Her loose-fitting tan blouse and polyester pants weren't exactly summery. "I've got an okay job as a receptionist and I manage the payments on my small house. But since my husband died two years ago, I don't feel like anybody needs me."

"That's a tough one." Bailey tried not to squirm on the hard bench.

"Aren't you going to tell me that life has meaning and I should get involved in something?" Renée unfolded her arms and rested them on the table.

"You might try dyeing your hair. That could perk you up." Most women in Southern California colored away the gray.

The older woman barked out a laugh. "That's ridiculous."

"It's a start," Bailey pointed out. "Work on the little things and the big ones will follow."

"Dyeing my hair won't make me matter to people."

Searching for a way to rouse the woman from her gloom, Bailey asked, "What do you think it would take? What *does* make one person matter to another?"

Renée's shoulders sank. "I'd feel differently if I had a child. I gave up my baby son for adoption when I was seventeen, before I met my husband."

"Maybe he'd like to meet you."

"I entered my name into one of those registries so he could find me, but he never has." Tears rimmed her eyes. "Does that shock you?"

"I'd think he would be curious," Bailey agreed.

"I mean, that I gave up my child." Renée gestured at Bailey's midsection. "You and your husband must be thrilled to death."

"Oh, I'm divorced—I'm carrying this for my sister," Bailey told her. "I'm probably going to end up just like you. Wait a minute—that sounded bad, didn't it?"

Renée gave a reluctant, almost painful chuckle. "It sounded horrible, but refreshing. At least you're honest. I hate having people patronize me. That's why I hardly ever talk to anyone."

Didn't the woman have *any* friends? Afraid of making her feel even worse, Bailey skipped that subject and returned to a neutral one. "There are websites where you can upload your picture and try out different hairstyles and hair colors."

"It sounds like fun," Renée conceded. "What color do you think would look good on me?"

Bailey considered. "Red, if you want to attract attention. Or you could go blond."

"And make a complete fool of myself?"

"How about strawberry-blond? That's subtle."

"I've been a mousy brown all my life. I don't think any shade of blond would be subtle." But Renée was smiling.

"If it doesn't work, you can always color over it."

The woman cocked her head as she considered. "You know what? I think I really might dye my hair. Although I don't see how that's going to change anything."

"If you have no purpose in life, that's kind of freeing," Bailey noted. "You could do anything you like. I mean, you could give your hair a purple stripe. Who's going to complain?"

"People sneer behind your back," Renée said.

"People sneer about me all the time, but as long as they do it behind my back, so what?" Bailey replied. "Half the hospital considers me nuts for being a surrogate, and they don't even know…well, never mind about that." Talking about her sister's laxness in paying medical bills could lead to a discussion of Bailey's current living circumstances, and she had more or less promised Owen to be discreet.

"Sounds like you could use a little counseling yourself," Renée observed.

"I'm a hopeless case." Bailey spotted Nora emerging from the annex. Sunlight turned the doctor's hair to spun gold, and a flowing rose-colored maternity top flattered her enlarged figure. "Wow, is it two o'clock already?"

Renée checked her watch. "So it is. I should have arrived sooner. You could have told me what color to paint my toenails."

"Wait till you pick a hair color," Bailey advised. "Then

you can coordinate that with your nails and maybe a new wardrobe."

Although it was a serious suggestion, Renée seemed amused. "I'll do that. Are you here every Saturday?"

"Depends." Bailey dug into her purse and found a business card with her cell number. "Call and I'll arrange to meet you."

Renée got to her feet. "You're a sweet person. I've enjoyed our talk."

"Me, too." Although she wasn't sure how much good she'd done, the woman did seem more cheerful.

While Renée strolled off, Bailey greeted Nora and went inside to sign out. She emerged to find the doctor lingering in the sunshine.

"I thought you'd left. Is Leo picking you up?" Even on a Saturday, he might be working across the street at the police station. Since his promotion to detective a few months ago, he'd been putting in long hours.

"Yes. He's running a few minutes late." Nora cleared her throat. "I was on call at the hospital this morning and heard some startling news."

"Oh?"

"Are you really sharing a house with Owen Tartikoff?"

Where had that information come from? Had Alec yakked to his colleagues? Her unwanted roomie was sure to blame the whole thing on Bailey. "Who told you that?"

"Rod Vintner, who was assisting at one of Owen's surgeries," she said. "Apparently the great Dr. T. made no bones about it."

"He told people?" What a hypocrite! "He practically bit my head off when he found out I'd discussed it with Patty."

"He's a control freak," Nora said. "As soon as he realized

word was bound to get out, he must have decided to manage the message."

Although there was still no sign of Leo, they headed down the gentle slope to the parking lot. They'd soon be rotund enough to roll rather than walk, Bailey mused.

"What exactly did you hear?" she asked.

"That he co-owns the house where your sister's letting you stay." Nora adjusted the shoulder strap of her purse. "And that Boone's his brother."

"Half brother," Bailey corrected.

"Were you aware of that? Before yesterday, I mean?"

"I had no idea."

Nora gazed wistfully toward the parking lot entrance. You could tell she and Leo were newlyweds, the way they missed each other when they were apart for more than five minutes. They hadn't been able to spare more than a weekend for a honeymoon because Leo needed to get up to speed on his new position. However, they'd be taking a ten-day trip to Hawaii in early August, which meant a bit of a break for Bailey, too.

"So Owen is your baby's uncle." Nora's voice broke into her reverie.

"Yeah. How about that?"

Nora clicked her tongue. "You don't have to put up with that man's bullying. Bailey, your sister had no business letting him move in without your consent. You didn't agree, did you?"

"Totally blindsided." Usually, Bailey enjoyed talking to Nora, but today she felt an urge to get away before anything awkward hit the fan. Anything *more* awkward.

"Tell Phyllis to put you up somewhere else," Nora said. "She's not paying you to be her surrogate. The least she can do is make sure you have decent living quarters."

"She can't afford it." Bailey clamped her mouth shut

too late. Why, oh, why hadn't she developed the habit of controlling her tongue?

Nora studied her with concern. "You told me your sister and brother-in-law were doing well financially."

"They are!" Bailey hurried to explain. "They've got a piece of a big construction project, a wonderful invest-ment opportunity in New Zealand, and they're pouring everything into it."

"You sound like you're quoting someone," Nora said skeptically.

Bailey hesitated, only for an instant, but the doctor must know her well enough to note the significance. After all, they'd worked together for five years. "That's what Phyllis said. But so what?"

"You're concerned and so am I." Beneath the pink top, something rippled. Was that the baby moving? At five months, it was possible—or Nora might just be breathing heavily. "Bailey, how much of your savings is invested with their firm?"

"About…twenty thousand dollars." To Bailey, it was an enormous sum.

"Is that everything you have?"

No use dissembling. "Pretty much."

Nora tapped her foot. "I'd hate to think of you losing it."

"I won't. They send me monthly accounting." Across the lot, a group of senior citizens emerged from the main building, exchanging farewells as they dispersed. They reminded her of something. "Most of their clients are older folks, like those guys. They're smart. I'm sure a lot of them have experience with investing. They must be staying on top of the whole business."

Nora's expression darkened. "How do they find these investors? Through seminars?"

"Yes. And word of mouth." Bailey had heard the whole spiel. "Seniors have the funds to invest, so naturally Phyllis and Boone go where the money is."

"This is making me very uncomfortable." Nora broke off as a red sports car veered off the street and navigated the parking lot toward them. "I should ask Leo to have someone check into it."

Sic the police on her sister? "You can't do that!" Bailey protested. "Casting doubt on their reputations—that could ruin them, even if they're innocent."

"You're not sure, though, are you? Why else would you say *if?*"

She didn't have an answer. Nora gave her a hug and slid into the car beside handsome, beaming Leo.

Was it possible she'd placed too much trust in her sister? Bailey wondered. But Phyllis wouldn't take advantage of her. No, if anything was wrong, it must be Boone's fault... only he was Dr. Tartikoff's brother. Surely *he* couldn't be guilty of anything underhanded, either.

Wait. Why was she defending the guy's honor, as if he had any? Owen had lectured her about keeping her mouth shut, then gone and blabbed to the entire operating room about them sharing a house. If not for that, Nora wouldn't have started poking into Bailey's affairs and there wouldn't be a risk of the cops becoming suspicious.

Bailey had to be angry at someone, and she couldn't blame Nora. She didn't want to target her sister, either. That left the man who'd shot his mouth off.

He deserved a piece of her mind. And tonight, she was going to give it to him.

OWEN SPENT SATURDAY AFTERNOON in L.A., taping a round-table discussion with a medical ethicist, a state assembly-man and a patients' rights advocate about how far doctors should go to comply with a patient's wishes in implanting multiple embryos. While everyone agreed that the health and safety of mother and babies were paramount, they disagreed about whether legislation should intervene.

As always, Owen enjoyed the fierce debate. He never lost his awareness, though, of the presence of TV cameras and the need to choose his words carefully.

The assemblyman argued in favor of legislation. "I plan to introduce a bill setting up a panel to establish standards for doctors in fertility cases," he announced.

"Just what we need, more bureaucrats intruding into women's private medical decisions!" the advocate flared. "A lot of states and foreign countries take a heavy-handed approach. Many of them bar surrogacy, as if women were imbeciles who can't make decisions for themselves. Thank goodness California hasn't gone that route!"

The mention of surrogates broke into Owen's concentration. Was there a need for regulation in that regard? As it stood, he wasn't the only one who'd been deceived; so had Bailey. Should there be ground rules about how much had to be disclosed? And if so, to whom—the woman, or the donor, too?

"Dr. Tartikoff?" prompted the moderator. "What do you think?"

Startled, he realized he'd lost track of the discussion. Rallying, Owen said, "The field of fertility is advancing rapidly. I consider it inadvisable to impose rigid rules or a government bureaucracy. What seems unreasonable or unsafe one year may be standard practice the next."

"Dr. Tartikoff raises a good point," the ethicist put in. "Also, it isn't good medicine to apply one-size-fits-all guidelines to such intensely personal cases."

Relieved at having ducked a curve ball, Owen stayed

attentive from then on. But his traitorous brain kept trying to stray to his own situation.

It disturbed him that he'd lost some of his objectivity. Fertility issues had never felt personal before, but they did now. He didn't like the fact that he—and apparently Bailey—had been tricked. And he had an ethical issue of his own to consider.

Namely, since he'd found out the truth, was he morally obligated to tell her?

With breaks for equipment checks and lighting adjustments, the discussion lasted far longer than the half hour that would air on the cable channel. Still, as he shook hands with his fellow panelists afterward, Owen considered it an afternoon well spent.

He had dinner with a colleague from UCLA, then drove back in rapidly falling darkness. The sprawling, flat landscape made him miss the green, rolling hills around Boston. On the other hand, he had to admit that, when he needed to merge through traffic, the drivers in Southern California were less likely to engage in bumper-to-bumper combat.

His thoughts flew to the evening ahead. On a Saturday in Boston, he might have attended a social event, but it wasn't unusual to return to a quiet house and an evening of catching up on medical journals. Tonight, he realized, he had no idea whether his house would be filled with Bailey's friends.

Or simply alive with her presence.

He pictured her curled on the couch, reading or watching TV. When he walked in, she'd slant him a glance full of mischief or possibly irritation. It would be fun matching wits with her. He might even plop down and insist on watching the rest of whatever chick flick she'd chosen, since it was his big-screen TV in the living room.

Bailey's Honda was hogging the single-width driveway and, in front of the house, an unfamiliar sedan blocked the curb. Owen found a space on the cul-de-sac and retrieved his briefcase from the trunk.

Wondering if she had a visitor or if the car belonged to a neighbor, he made his way through predatory palm fronds to the front door. Didn't his brother employ a gardener for this place? Also, half the low Malibu lights along the walk were burned out. For the past year, Boone hadn't paid Owen any proceeds from the rent, claiming it all went to the mortgage, insurance, upkeep and repairs. What repairs had been done, exactly?

From inside came the sweet soaring notes of a favorite song, "If I Loved You" from *Carousel*. A sucker for Rodgers and Hammerstein musicals, Owen paused on the porch to enjoy the lovely alto voice and the simple piano arrangement. He didn't recognize the recording…and then he heard a sour note on the piano and realized it wasn't a recording. Not a piano, either, but a keyboard, judging by the tone.

The music stopped. He heard a man say, "You can't quit now!"

Even though Owen agreed, he felt a flash of disappointment. Bailey hadn't mentioned a boyfriend.

"I'm not quitting!" she challenged. "You were supposed to join in."

"It's the wrong key," the guy protested.

"You're just making excuses."

"That's true. I prefer listening to you. With a voice like that, you could have been a…"

"Nurse," Bailey finished, and they both laughed.

Gritting his teeth, Owen turned the key and let himself in. Across the open main room, at the gleaming mahogany dining table, Bailey sat behind a keyboard. Next to her, a deeply tanned blond fellow leaned close, beaming.

With a start, Owen recognized Ned Norwalk, the nurse he'd bossed around at the hospital today. And judging by Ned's narrowed eyes as he looked up, the guy wouldn't mind getting payback.

Much as it galled Owen, he'd better watch what he said. It might get repeated at work. "Good evening." That seemed safe enough.

Ned ducked his head in grudging recognition. Bailey tapped a note on the keyboard. "You can close your door if the music bothers you."

"I'll do that."

He didn't mind the music itself, Owen reflected as he strode through and shut himself into his room. But what on earth made Ned think his tenor was worthy of joining Bailey in "Edelweiss"? If those two planned further duets in the bedroom, he'd have to put in his earplugs, Owen grumbled as he set his laptop on his desk.

He should be the one singing with Bailey. In high school, he'd starred in several musicals, and had performed roles in college productions, as well. He was eons better than that idiot Ned.

But on his home territory, he'd just been one-upped. And for tonight, there wasn't a damn thing he could do about it.

Chapter Five

Usually, Bailey liked to stay up late, especially on the weekend, and songfests were among her favorite activities. Tonight, though, she caught herself drooping by 10:00 p.m.

"I can hardly keep my eyes open," she told Ned as she sat in the kitchen, watching him fix ice cream sundaes. "It's ridiculously early."

Through an open window above the sink, a welcome breeze played over her. That revived her a little, but she could feel a whole series of yawns backed up like cars at a stop sign.

"You're pregnant. You need your sleep. And your calcium and potassium." He set a bowl in front of her. Bananas, vanilla ice cream, caramel topping, peanut sprinkles. Mmm. "Also, you're big for your date, as I'm sure you know. That doctor in L.A. really isn't concerned?"

"I'm fine." Bailey toyed with the notion of admitting the truth and persuading Ned to give her a checkup, but she hated to confide such an intimate family matter. Also, he wasn't a nurse practitioner, and she didn't want to involve him in anything that might boomerang on him.

Her friend had already had one dustup with Owen today, she'd learned. Judging by the glare Dr. T. had cast in their direction earlier, it wouldn't take much to bring down his wrath on Ned's hapless head.

"You ought to be living with someone who cares about you." Bringing over his own sundae, Ned took a seat.

"You volunteering?" she teased, although they didn't have that kind of relationship. She liked Ned too much as a friend to get romantic, and besides, they'd never struck any sparks. The problem was, the men who set off chemical reactions with her tended to flame hotly and then burn out, leaving the taste of ashes in her mouth.

Ned glanced toward the living room, although there'd been no sign of Owen for at least an hour. "If he weren't here, I'd offer to move in. You know you can count on me if you need anything."

"Of course." Impulsively, she asked, "Are you unhappy at work? You told me you weren't enjoying being a surgical nurse as much as you expected."

"I like being part of a team, and it's miraculous what a good surgeon can accomplish." He paused to enjoy a mouthful of ice cream before continuing. "But I miss forming a relationship with the patients. They're too groggy to notice me, and then I never see them again."

"It's more fun being in an office," Bailey agreed. "You could transfer. There'll be some new doctors joining the staff, so there should be openings."

"I might do that."

After they finished eating, he rinsed the bowls, loaded the dishwasher and turned it on. What a considerate guy, Bailey reflected as they said good-night. Ned had everything Owen lacked: kindness, humility, dependability. She wouldn't trust Dr. T. to put anyone's interests ahead of his own. He did take care of his own dishes, she conceded, but that was no doubt due to a surgeon's dislike for germs.

Barely able to set one foot ahead of the other, Bailey went to bed. Her hormones must have put her into a near-coma almost instantly, because the next thing she knew, she awoke to diffused, early morning light filtering through the blinds.

One of Southern California's occasional spells of summer gloom, with overcast skies and temperatures dropping into the fifties overnight, had arrived this weekend. What a perfect morning for a dip in the hot tub. She didn't use it nearly as much as she'd expected to, and she might not get many more chances before summer's heat struck in earnest.

Now, what did a strapped-for-cash pregnant lady wear to the spa? Bailey hadn't wanted to spend money on a maternity swimsuit and she wasn't about to go out in a bikini, even in her fenced rear yard, so she pulled on a pair of loose shorts, a T-shirt and flip-flops. That ought to serve well enough.

For breakfast, she finished off the last banana with her cereal. She was collecting a beach towel from the linen closet when it occurred to her that the sliding-glass exit to the patio lay in Owen's bedroom. The alternative was to go out the front door and fight her way through the odds and ends in the side yard.

How inconvenient. Besides, either he was already awake or he'd put in earplugs and might not even notice her. Why should she go to a lot of trouble on his behalf?

The closed door to Owen's room presented a forbidding obstacle. Refusing to be daunted, Bailey tapped lightly, turned the handle and peered inside.

Dark wood furnishings crowded the room, and firmly shut vertical blinds blocked almost all the light. In the high, old-fashioned bed, a large shape lay under a heavy quilt that rose and fell gently. The scents of aftershave lotion and male hormones, or whatever the man exuded, filled her nostrils. Pregnancy had made her ultrasensitive to smells, but she didn't find the odors unpleasant. In fact, she got a little buzz.

She did *not* have chemistry with this man. No way.

Pressing her lips together, she ventured inside. Why did it have to be so dark in here? She expected at any moment to stumble over a pair of his shoes, but the carpet was mercifully uncluttered. Oh, right. Control freak surgeons probably lined up their shoes in their closets, color coordinated with their suits.

Reaching the glass door, Bailey faced her next challenge: she couldn't exit without rattling the blinds as she pushed them aside. True, it might be fun to crash her way out and close the door with a thump, just to test the quality of the man's earplugs and be as pesky as possible. He deserved it for snapping at Ned yesterday. Didn't he see how unfair it was to pick on people who couldn't fight back?

Common sense won. If she meant to relax in the spa, she'd better not wake the man. So, as quietly as she could, Bailey bunched the slats in one hand, unlocked and slid open the door, and scooted outside.

A BURST OF COOL AIR WOKE Owen, followed by a vibration as if someone had shut a door or window. He blinked in the dim light, taking a moment to recall where he was and why he couldn't hear anything.

When he removed the earplugs, he heard a whooshing noise from outside. The jets in the spa, he assumed.

Had Bailey sneaked through his bedroom to get there? Of course she had. But surely she didn't have the nerve to bring her boyfriend tromping through here, as well. That would be pushing her luck.

If she pushed, he'd push back, harder.

Owen showered, shaved and put on the sleek blue swim

trunks he'd bought for the move to California. He hadn't yet joined an exercise club, but he planned to.

With the blinds drawn, he couldn't see what was going on outside. He couldn't hear voices, either, but that might be due to the rumble of the Jacuzzi jets. How awkward if he stepped out and surprised the two of them in flagrante delicto.

Giving no warning, Owen yanked on the blinds and opened the slider. In the round tub, Bailey's lightly freckled face turned toward him. She blinked as if coming out of a pleasant daze.

No sign of anyone else in the tub or on the patio. Just a screen of ferns and palms, and a couple of tall, tropical bushes covered with orange and pink blossoms. "What happened to Nurse Nelly?" he inquired as he threw his towel over a lawn chair.

"You mean Ned?"

"I was referring to the nurse in *South Pacific*." He hadn't intended to be rude. Much.

"You don't have to act like a total jerk about him," Bailey retorted. "He's had a tough life."

Owen had never considered what kind of life a male nurse led, one way or another. He didn't care to mention that to Bailey and spark another biting comment. "Is that so?"

"You should admire him for earning his RN. Hold on. It's too noisy in here." She reached out to turn off the jets, seemingly unaware of how the T-shirt stretched tantalizingly across her breasts. "He got bounced around from one relative's home to another, growing up. Not everyone comes from a privileged background."

Forcing his gaze away from her nearly transparent T-shirt, Owen slid into the water. Pleasantly warm but, as she'd mentioned, not hot enough to endanger the fetus. "Privileged? My mother was a cleaning lady."

"You're kidding!" She sat upright, as if challenging him.

"Nope." He rarely told anyone.

A few seconds passed before she apparently accepted that he wasn't going to retract his statement. "Boone never mentioned that."

"Has he said much about our family?"

"Just that his parents are dead. I didn't even realize he had a half brother." At least she'd quit glaring since Owen had revealed his mother's occupation. "You had different fathers, right?"

"Yes." *Very* different.

"What was his dad like?"

"I gather he had some trouble with the law." The man had been in and out of prison and had died there, but Owen saw no point in revealing that. "He was a…businessman." Of the grifter persuasion.

"What did your father do?" Bailey asked.

"He edited a newspaper for fellow Russian dissidents who'd fled to the U.S." It was a well-known fact, but Owen found himself going beyond that. "As you can imagine, it didn't pay well. Soviet prison camps destroyed his health, so he couldn't do much else."

"That must have been tough on you."

"When I was a kid, I simply accepted my parents' circumstances. Sure, I wished we were rich, but we got by." His parents had loved and encouraged him, which was more than a lot of children experienced. In a way, Owen supposed, he *had* been privileged.

"How'd you get through medical school?" Bailey brushed back a curly strand of damp hair.

"Scholarships. Loans. Summer research internships." He leaned back, letting the warm water soothe him, and hoped he wasn't talking too much. On his résumé and in person, Owen preferred to show himself to advantage. Revealing your weaknesses opened you to people's condescension.

But Bailey, who'd stretched along the underwater ledge that served as a bench, wasn't sneering. "So neither you nor Boone grew up rich."

Owen's mouth stretched into an ironic smile. "No. We weren't that close, by the way. He was seven when our parents married, and eight when I was born, so by the time I reached junior high, he was already out on his own."

"Getting his MBA, right?" Bailey said.

Owen doubted his brother had earned that degree. "He took business classes at NYU."

"While you went to Harvard."

"Yale, undergrad. Then Harvard Medical School. On scholarships, as I said." Usually Owen didn't mind showing off, but with Bailey, he seemed to make more headway when he confessed his weaknesses.

Headway? He had no agenda with her. In fact, the last thing he sought was any entanglement with a nurse at the medical center, especially one with whom he shared a house.

And who was carrying his baby.

His gaze slid instinctively to her rounded abdomen. There was something deliciously sensual about her pregnancy-enhanced shape. Must be some ancient instinctive male attraction to fertility, especially since there was part of him inside there.

Best to avoid the subject. But how could he resist? Besides, as the supposed uncle, he had an excuse to be curious. "Why did you agree to be your sister's surrogate?"

Bailey's eyebrows drew up in a wonderfully schoolmarmish expression. "Exactly how did you segue from medical school to my baby bump?"

"Just answer the question," Owen said.

"Because she needed me." Without pausing to let him ask anything further, Bailey volleyed, "My turn! Why did you decide to work with infertile women? You don't seem like the warm fuzzy type."

She had a frustrating talent for throwing Owen off balance. He wished he had a simple explanation, but the truth was more complicated. "Let's start with the fact that I'm interested in using my skill as a surgeon to improve people's lives. I considered other specialties."

"Such as?"

He thought back to his days in medical school. "Cardiac surgery, for one. My father died of a heart attack, but he'd been weakened by starvation, and surgery couldn't have fixed that."

"I'm sorry," Bailey said. "And you lost your mom, too."

"To cancer. She didn't even tell me she was ill, so I never got to share her battle." His breath caught at the memory. Why was he getting emotional about a loss that had happened a decade ago? "By then I was doing my residency in obstetrics."

"You still haven't told me why you chose that field," she persisted.

Owen hadn't reviewed his reasons for a long time. "I suppose that after all the death and suffering my parents went through, I chose a field filled with hope. I'd more or less forgotten that along the way. Thanks for reminding me."

"Wow. I can't believe what I'm learning about you," she said. "You sound halfway human."

"Don't strain yourself paying me compliments."

She stuck out her feet and wiggled her toes. "I promise not to ruin your reputation as a grouch."

Her toenails were painted lavender, Owen noticed, and

wondered how much longer she'd be able to reach them, at the rate her baby was growing. "That's big of you. Literally." Without pausing to think, he blurted, "Why does Phyllis need a surrogate?"

"She's forty."

"That isn't old for a maternity patient these days. What else?"

Bailey regarded him aslant, as if weighing whether to trust him. "Well, you *are* part of the family, so I guess it's no secret. After she had a couple of miscarriages, her doctor diagnosed something called Inherited Chromosomal Rearrangements. I guess you know what that is."

"I do." In two to four percent of cases involving repeated miscarriages, one of the parents turned out to have an unusual structure of chromosomes. These didn't affect the parent because the translocated chromosomes were balanced, with no missing or extra pieces, but when they were passed to the child, pieces might go astray. The result could be severe birth defects or miscarriage. While such parents had a chance of producing healthy children, Owen understood why a forty-year-old woman who'd had several miscarriages might give up. "You didn't inherit the condition?"

"Luckily, no."

"So you're using your eggs, not hers?"

She nodded.

Neither Boone *nor* Phyllis had contributed DNA, which meant that this baby's parents were both right here. Until a few days ago, they'd been strangers, and after the birth they'd merely be the child's aunt and uncle, but right now they were, in a sense, primary.

"Did you take fertility drugs?" he asked.

"Why do you ask?"

He wished she'd stop skirting the issue. "Because you're big for three months."

"It looks that way because I'm short."

Who did she think she was talking to? "I'm an expert. You're large for your dates."

"No fertility drugs. I didn't need them."

"That's good." Still, he had the sense she was holding back. "And you're getting regular checkups?"

"Well..." Her lips parted, and she studied him as if struggling with a decision.

What was going on? "Tell me."

"Did I mention why Phyllis is letting me stay here? I mean, aside from the fact that I'm her surrogate?"

He didn't see the connection. "What does this house have to do with anything?"

"I'm working up to it!" Bailey flared.

"Just get to the point." Seeing her frown, Owen struggled to rein in his impatience. "Sorry. Tell me in your own way." Forcing himself to relax, he sprawled out in the water, elbows on the concrete lip, legs brushing hers lightly. If he had to humor her, he might as well get comfortable.

And if his body insisted on responding in ways that could be embarrassing in a skimpy swimsuit, he hoped she was too preoccupied to notice.

Chapter Six

How much should I tell him? On most topics, Bailey talked freely to her friends—perhaps too freely, she'd been advised more than once. She'd already spilled too much about her sister and brother-in-law's financial dealings to Nora, for instance.

Yet within a family, people had to trust each other, and Owen was part of the family. Furthermore, his comment echoed her own concerns. When she'd agreed to have a baby for Phyllis, she'd committed to doing everything in her power to sustain a healthy pregnancy. She certainly hadn't expected to have to proceed without proper medical care.

The man watching her from across the small pool didn't seem like the overbearing Dr. Tartikoff. When he'd discussed his parents' hardships, she'd seen the pain and recognized how much dedication it had taken to achieve his success. This wasn't some spoiled golden boy. He was the baby's uncle, and a world-class obstetrician. It would be wrong to let pride stand in the way of doing her duty to her baby.

"As I said, we didn't use fertility drugs," she began. "I guess we would have if I hadn't become pregnant right away, but Phyllis didn't want to spend more than necessary and I was happy to avoid the risk of side effects."

"Do twins run in your family?" Despite the fact that he was half-naked and his ankle kept brushing her thigh, he projected the calm assessment of a physician. Quite a trick, in Bailey's opinion.

"Not as far as I know. But there are other reasons why I could be so big. I mean, size is relative…" She broke off, aware that she was making a hash of this.

The water swished as he sat up. "You're telling me you haven't had an ultrasound?"

"I was leading up to that," Bailey conceded. "The reason I'm living here is that Phyllis and Boone are having this cash flow problem. I was fronting the money for the doctor bills, only I couldn't afford that anymore. When the renter moved out, my sister offered to let me live here as compensation."

"They're broke?" Concern and anger flashed across Owen's face.

"Not broke!" They couldn't be. They were managing her lifesavings, and a lot of other people's, too. Besides, Phyllis wouldn't lie to her. "It's just that funds are temporarily tight, that's all."

Owen leaned forward. "When was the last time you had a checkup?"

She couldn't keep dodging the truth. "Six weeks ago."

He smacked the water with his palm, splashing them both. "Of all the irresponsible…"

"I didn't confide in you so you could criticize me!" Bailey might have slammed water right back in his face, except that this was far too serious a matter for roughhousing.

"Not you. Boone and your sister." Owen scowled past her, as if visualizing his brother. "They had no business commissioning you as a surrogate if they're in a financial bind. Let alone taking you to some clinic in L.A., and then neglecting to pay for your treatment."

Hearing her worries put into words gave Bailey a sick feeing in the pit of her stomach. "What's done is done," she said miserably. "I'm carrying their child. I just have to make the best of it. Besides, Phyllis and I grew up without any money. Poor people deserve to have children, too."

"They don't deserve to talk their trusting sister into bearing a child for them! Especially when…" He stopped in midsentence. "This is getting us nowhere. Let's go give you a checkup."

"What?" She hadn't expected *him* to offer. "I should ask Nora."

His jaw clenched. Why on earth did he care? Being an uncle didn't exactly make him intimately involved, and Bailey doubted that the formidable Dr. T. had performed an ultrasound on a patient in years. While obstetricians were trained to do them, most assigned the job to a technician.

"You said yourself this is a family matter," he said tightly. "If there's a problem, I'll help you deal with it."

Bailey wasn't sure how to react. In her experience, men didn't take care of you. They stuck around for the fun and games, and then made themselves scarce. Obviously, Owen had a strong sense of responsibility about his brother's failure to provide for her.

"You mean right now?" she asked.

"Sure. I've got a key to the office." He arose, dripping, an impressive sight from her angle. Lots of muscles, a hard stomach and…why was she looking at that part of his anatomy? "Need a hand up?"

"I can manage." She braced on the pool's lip and levered herself upright.

Owen might be doing her a favor this once, but she didn't intend to start counting on a guy for support, literally or figuratively. Because despite his generosity, he'd soon get distracted by more pressing matters.

Men always did.

As A CHILD, OWEN HAD ADORED his smart, slick, fast-talking older brother. Boone had sheltered him in return, coming to his aid in junior high when a bully at school repeatedly taunted Owen, stole his badly needed lunch money and trashed his backpack. After complaints to the principal's office failed to resolve the problem, Boone had paid the school a visit and managed—he'd never disclosed the details—to plant marijuana in the guy's locker and get him transferred to a program for troubled students.

A couple of years ago, when his brother discovered that he suffered from a low sperm count, Owen hadn't hesitated to donate his own. And although Boone should have informed Owen about the decision to use a surrogate, that might not have been a deliberate deception.

But this financial business was troubling. Boone's father had been convicted of operating confidence games that stole hundreds of thousands of dollars from naive investors. Was Boone following in his father's footsteps right here in Safe Harbor?

As he finished drying off in the bedroom, Owen wrestled with that possibility. If Boone and Phyllis were abusing their investors' trust, how would that affect Bailey? If they got arrested, how badly was that going to reflect on Owen and the fertility program? Most important, should he notify the police of his suspicions?

He had no proof and no real evidence, he conceded as he pulled on a polo shirt. Boone and his wife's failure to arrange for proper medical care was a serious matter, but hardly criminal. If someone reported Owen to the police on vague suspicions, endangering his reputation and his medical license, he'd be furious and consider filing a libel suit.

Let sleeping dogs lie, his mother used to say. When she was out of the room, Owen's father had added, *But never turn your back on them.* Both pieces of advice struck him as worthwhile in this situation.

Deciding to leave the matter alone for the moment, Owen zipped up his jeans and slid his bare feet into a pair of loafers. Right now, he had to make sure Bailey and her baby were all right.

His baby, too. Not that he'd ever tell anyone. But how miraculous to be the first person to actually see it.

Owen kept up his skills by performing occasional ultrasounds, and he'd always enjoyed the parents' reactions. Today, he was going to discover how that felt in an entirely new way.

THERE WAS AN EERIE EMPTINESS to the Safe Harbor Medical Building on a Sunday, Bailey noticed as Owen let them into a first-floor corridor through a side door. Despite the July sunshine outside, dimness bathed the hallway, with only faint safety lights to guide the way. When they entered the lobby, no one sat behind the reception desk to check them in, and the pharmacy was shuttered.

She shivered. "Cold?" Owen asked.

"No. It just seems strange, with no one around."

"We're around." Giving her a crooked grin, he punched the elevator button.

Bailey wasn't even close to feeling cold, and not only because of her pregnancy hormones. Owen seemed to be generating waves of energy, or maybe it was his dark red hair that gave the illusion of heat. Around him, she felt herself glowing like a furnace.

When he ushered her into the mirrored elevator, she

felt a glimmer of doubt. Much as she needed an exam, maybe she should beg off and wait until she could see another obstetrician. Then she wouldn't have to undress for this guy.

He's a doctor. Yes, and she was a nurse. Wasn't that a game couples played? *Let's go into a room where you can examine me.*

Bailey summoned her nerve as the doors opened at the third floor. "I'm not sure this is proper."

"Proper?" Owen stood aside to let her out. "What a quaint term."

"I meant…" What *did* she mean? "You don't have my medical records. And you're my brother-in-law, kind of. And besides…" *Shut up, Bailey.*

"And besides, we're here, so let's go." Taking her elbow, Owen guided her around a corner to a door marked with his name and specialties. Obstetrics, gynecology, fertility. None of that came close to summing up the tall, hard and overwhelmingly confident man beside her. "This is strictly between you, me and the baby. I assure you, I don't plan to become your regular physician."

The waiting room was much like Nora's a floor below, except that the couches and the paint smelled new. The place had obviously been refurbished for its star occupant.

"I don't care how private this is," Bailey protested. "I'm nervous."

Owen switched on the light, closed the door and folded his arms. "About my qualifications?"

"Of course not!"

"Glad to hear it." With another of those cocky grins, he led the way to the inner suite.

Bailey's hand drifted to her midsection. "I'm not ready."

Owen flicked on the overheads in an examining room.

"I'm only going to listen to the baby's heartbeat and perform an ultrasound. There's nothing invasive."

"It's not the medical procedure."

"Then what?"

This was hard to admit. "I'm not ready for the baby to be real."

At the sink, he washed his hands. "How's that?"

Bailey struggled to summon the right words, for herself as well as for him. "When I volunteered to be a surrogate, I had this vague idea of my sister holding a baby and humming lullabies, like in some commercial. Sure, I knew I'd get big and suffer nausea and backaches, and that eventually the little guy would have to come out of me, but it was all kind of remote."

"So you'd rather watch a greeting card commercial than see your own baby on an ultrasound?"

Bailey glared. "I shouldn't have expected you to understand. It's not like it's your kid."

From a cabinet, Owen took out a hospital gown, the latest model in powder-blue. Nora's patients made do with much-laundered pink gowns. "Put this on. I'll be back in a sec."

"You aren't listening!"

"You want to change in front of me?" One eyebrow arched. "I'm game."

She accepted the gown. "I'll talk to Nora tomorrow. There's no reason for you to do this."

"Other than the fact that we're here?" He looked much larger than usual in this intimate room.

"If we go home, we won't be here," Bailey countered. "That will take care of that."

He started to laugh. "You're a tough character."

She narrowed her eyes. "And you're stubborn as an ox."

Gently, he reached out and rubbed his palms across her

shoulders. "You're scared. This whole situation feels out of control, right?"

His kind tone caught her off guard. "I didn't expect to get pregnant right away," Bailey blurted. "Then, after I did, Phyllis more or less abandoned me. I mean, about the medical care. Now I'm sticking out to here already, which means there might be something wrong."

Owen leaned down, his forehead close to hers. "Let's not get ahead of ourselves. The fact that you're large doesn't mean there's a problem. That's what we're here to learn."

To Bailey's embarrassment, tears burned in her eyes. "What if I see the baby and it isn't…I don't know…"

"One step at a time," he murmured.

Bailey felt an irrational urge to cling to Owen. A woman needed the father with her during a pregnancy. She'd blindly accepted the assurance that her sister would fill that role, but now she was left counting on a man she hardly knew. And he was being so gentle. If she weren't careful, she'd put her arms around him. This was Dr. Owen Tartikoff! Was she out of her mind?

Pride, more than anything, enabled her to draw a deep breath and straighten her shoulders. "Okay. I'll change."

He nodded, but stayed right where he was, close enough for her to smell his aftershave lotion and that indefinable *essence de Owen.*

"You can step out now, Doctor," Bailey said with a touch of sharpness. "I'll push the button when I'm ready." That would activate a green light in the hallway.

"Thank you, Nurse." Looking amused, he strode out.

Bailey made a face at the blue gown in her arms. Was she actually going to let her know-it-all roommate put his hands all over her?

Might as well get this over with. Because no matter how

frightened she was of what the ultrasound might reveal, she had to find out what was going on.

Since Owen loathed wasting time, he leaned against the counter at the nurses' station and checked Monday's schedule in his phone. Surgery, appointments, a staff meeting that he'd called, a phone interview with one of the more promising fellowship applicants. He started making notes, but his mind kept drifting away.

What if there *was* something amiss?

He shook his head at his foolishness. If a problem existed, most likely it could be treated. He handled neonatal complications all the time, and while he understood parents' natural anxiety, usually they worried for nothing.

Owen began to pace. What was taking Bailey so long? She didn't seem like the type to fold her clothes with military precision.

The light remained red.

At thirteen weeks' gestation, the fetus was fully formed from its fingers to its toes. He couldn't count the number of times he'd run over the facts with expectant parents, but today everything felt different. In just a few minutes, he'd be witnessing a miracle. His miracle. His and Bailey's.

With a start, Owen realized he'd forgotten to fetch the sonogram equipment and went down the hall to retrieve it from a cabinet. The entire machine, complete with computer screen and keyboard, fit neatly onto a cart, which he wheeled back toward the examining room.

The light was still red. After a split second's internal debate, he tapped on the door. "You okay?"

"Oh!" A scrabbling noise, and the light changed to green.

He opened the door. "You forgot?" How was that possible? She dealt with patients and their stop-go lights every day.

"I was distracted." Sitting on the examining table, Bailey pulled the dressing gown tightly around her.

To Owen's dismay, he had to deliberately block out an awareness of her rounded breasts beneath the cloth. However temporarily, Bailey was his patient, and he had no business getting aroused. He'd never, ever crossed the line between being a doctor and being a man. Never allowed himself to be tempted.

Had she been right? Was this improper?

Oh, just get on with it.

Positioning the cart to one side, he lifted the Doppler stethoscope from the wall. This microphone-like device also used sound waves, in this case to represent the fetal heartbeat. "You can position it yourself if you prefer."

Bailey practically snatched the stethoscope from his hand and slid it through the front gap in her gown. "I don't hear a heartbeat!" She stared at him in alarm.

Owen chuckled. "Try moving it until you find the right place."

She blushed. "I knew that. But I thought this *was* the right place. Okay, okay." She shifted the device. Still nothing. Owen fought the impulse to grab the stethoscope and position it with practiced skill.

And then, from a small speaker on the wall, whooshing noises filled the room, galloping like a runaway horse. Fast, but no more than normal for a fetus at this stage.

"Wow." Bailey's wide gaze met his. "It's strong."

Owen could hardly swallow. Yes, it was. Strong enough to last for decades, perhaps to keep on beating for a century. It was the sound of the future.

He'd described the heartbeat in similar terms for countless parents, and smiled at their wondering reactions. Now a fresh sense of awe spread through him. His child. What kind of person would it become? What kind of life would it lead?

With an effort, Owen remembered why they'd come here. "Move it some more," he said.

"Why?" Her nose wrinkled. "Oh." She shifted the device, and they both heard the same thing.

Another galloping horse in the background.

"Could that be an echo?" Bailey asked.

Enough of halfway measures. "Let's find out for sure," Owen said, removing the stethoscope and switching on the sonogram machine.

His gut tightened. Because for just a moment, in the rush of noises, he'd imagined he heard a little voice whispering, "Hello, Daddy."

Or had that been two little voices?

Chapter Seven

Twins. Even though she'd known that was possible, Bailey couldn't believe it. Yes, twins could and did occur without fertility drugs, both the identical and the fraternal types, but she hadn't expected it.

Phyllis with two babies. A girl for her, a boy for Boone? Or were they both the same sex?

As she lay back on the table and let Owen spread gel on her stomach, Bailey tried to picture her sister and brother-in-law getting up at night to change two sets of diapers. Playing with a pair of toddlers under the Christmas tree. Shooting video as the kids raced up the walkway to their first day at school.

They kept fading from the picture. It was Bailey soothing a crying infant and helping rip the colorful paper from holiday presents, Bailey who held the camera to her eye, capturing that key moment. And beside her...would there ever be a man beside her?

"There's baby number one." The pressure on her stomach and the sound of Owen's voice snatched Bailey from her reflections.

"Can you tell the sex?" Even though she knew perfectly well that was unlikely at this early stage, she longed for an answer.

He peered closely at the screen. "Not close enough to

call it. Okay, baby number two, please come out from behind the curtain."

"This isn't a game!"

"Then why are you smiling?"

"Because I was pretending for a minute that they were really mine."

Although she braced for a smart-aleck comment, Owen kept his attention on the fluid black-and-white shapes pulsing on the screen. "Here we go. Baby number two. Active little guy, isn't he? Or she. They'd better enjoy themselves while they still have room to maneuver. When they get bigger, they'll be poking their elbows into you and each other."

"You don't have to tell me that," she groused, mostly because she wanted to vent at someone.

"Sorry. Most patients enjoy my little jokes."

"I'm not enjoying anything about this."

That wasn't true. Bailey had never seen anything more beautiful or amazing than the two precious bundles of life she carried inside her.

This ought to be a wonderful moment. Phyllis should be here brimming with delight. Boone ought to have his arm around his wife's waist as they eagerly followed the infants' activity.

We could have invited them today. But they had a standing invitation to accompany her to checkups. While Phyllis had gone with her to the first visit, Boone hadn't bothered, and neither had been present for the second.

The growing sense that she'd put her trust in the wrong people scared the heck out of Bailey. How was she going to entrust two helpless infants to parents who already had a poor track record when it came to parenting?

Yet she didn't see a choice. Even if she had some way to raise two babies on her own, she couldn't get out of this.

She'd signed an ironclad contract. Well, considering these were her eggs, perhaps not entirely ironclad, but because the babies would be Boone's genetic children. Did she really want to spend the rest of her life sharing custody with her brother-in-law, not to mention incurring what would no doubt be her sister's undying hatred?

A deal's a deal. That was practically the Wayne family motto. As kids, she and Phyllis had learned not to strike a bargain with their mother and then try to renegotiate. After complaining about their mom's hit-or-miss cooking, a twelve-year-old Bailey had boasted that she could do better, and accepted a challenge to cook dinner every night for a month. Her mother had held her to the deal, even though by the end they were eating cheese toast and canned spaghetti most nights. Come to think of it, that had been what they frequently ate when her Mom was cooking, too.

Owen continued to slide the probe across Bailey's bulge, pressing harder than seemed necessary. "It's incredible that sound waves can produce a picture from inside you, isn't it?"

"It's even more incredible that you can go on poking me like an unripe melon," Bailey grumbled. "What are you doing?"

"Trying to find baby number three. If there is one."

She nearly stopped breathing. "Triplets?"

More pressure. "Nope. Looks like nature stopped at the pair of them. Got any names picked out?"

"That isn't up to me, remember?"

"Force of habit." He paused the probe, pressed a button and printed out an image. "Everything looks good with the umbilical cord. Two separate placentas."

"So they're fraternal."

"Not necessarily." He went on to explain that while

identical twins could share a placenta, that wasn't always the case.

He didn't stop there. As he captured more images, he elaborated that two-thirds of twins were fraternal, and that while most of the remaining third were identical, in rare instances a woman might have half-identical twins. This occurred when a single egg split into two halves, which were then fertilized by separate sperm. These babies shared about seventy-five percent of their genetic markers, Owen said. Full identicals shared one hundred percent and fraternals had fifty percent in common, the same as singleton siblings.

"Why are you telling me this?" Bailey demanded.

He gave her a startled glance. "Don't you find it fascinating?"

"No!" Why hadn't she considered the possibility of complications before she leaped into surrogacy? Grimly, she stared up at him. "Carrying twins requires extra medical attention, and extra expense."

"Which is why you should start using a doctor on staff here." Removing the device, Owen wiped her stomach with a disposable towel. "I can help arrange that."

Under other circumstances, Bailey might have been impressed with his willingness to go to such lengths. At the moment, however, she had no energy to spare for anything except her own turbulent emotions. "I have to talk to Phyllis. About it being twins and…everything."

"I'll go with you." He was smearing as much gel as he removed.

Sitting up, Bailey snatched the towelette and finished removing the goop. "You mean now?"

"Can't think of a better time."

She wasn't sure she wanted this opinionated male intruding into a touchy situation. On the other hand, the discovery that she carried two babies threatened to overwhelm Bailey's reserve of confidence. As a nurse, she knew all too well that behind the happy baby pictures lay months of extra tests and added discomforts, as well as the increased likelihood of a Cesarean birth.

What would it hurt, this once, to have a man by her side? Obviously he wasn't *her* man, but for the moment he served as her doctor. Also, they were related. And, she reminded herself, it was her sister and brother-in-law's fault that Owen had intruded into her home, which was how he'd become involved in the first place.

"Okay. But remember, you're only along for moral support." Bailey adjusted her gown to cover her bare stomach. "I'm taking the lead and you can back me up with a few medical facts. Got it?"

Owen gave her a mock salute. "Yes, boss." She couldn't see his expression after that because he turned and wheeled the cart out of the room.

But she thought he was grinning.

Typical for Sunday, boats of all sizes and stripes filled Safe Harbor as Owen escorted Bailey to his brother's door. Was it really only two days since he'd come here for the first time, anticipating the sight of his sister-in-law's pregnant figure?

He hadn't even known Bailey existed. Now, not only did they share a house, they shared a legacy.

At the office, as he'd checked out the babies' miniature noses and perfect little arms and legs, he'd felt an irrational urge to talk to them. *Who are you guys? What kind of people will you be? Where are you going in life?*

And he'd started to get concerned about what kind of father Boone would be. The guy's dad hadn't been a great role model. You could pretty much count on Mr. Storey missing his arranged visits. Birthdays and holidays were the same, with Boone moping around, waiting for a dad who never showed. The next day, there might be a phone call filled with excuses. Other times, nothing for months.

But Owen hadn't thought about that when he agreed to his brother's request. He hadn't given any thought to the child or children that might result. And he hadn't visualized a mother like Bailey, alternately sweet and snappish, tenderhearted and bristling with indignation.

Whether she liked it or not, he considered her under his protection.

On the phone, Phyllis had sounded worried when Owen called to say he and Bailey needed to see the two of them. Boone had gone out of town for a few days, she'd informed him. Couldn't they postpone this?

When he said it was important, he'd heard the alarm in her voice. *You didn't tell her...?* No, he'd said, glad he was making the call from his office while Bailey dressed, so he could speak freely. It had nothing to do with his paternity.

He pressed the chimes a second time. "Big house," Bailey said. "Takes a while to get to the door."

"She's expecting us. It shouldn't take that long."

"Don't start criticizing my sister!" Bailey's jaw set stubbornly.

Owen reined in his impatience. "All right."

"And remember to let me take the lead," she added. "The surrogacy is between me, Phyllis and Boone. Uncles don't have rights. Got it?"

If you only knew. Again, he flirted with the notion that he ought to tell her. Full disclosure, especially considering how much they were sharing.

But even though Bailey didn't know the whole story, she had a point: this wasn't his battle. He'd given his sperm freely, without conditions. And cute as those tiny babies were, he wasn't prepared to take responsibility for raising them.

He caught the now-familiar slap of sandals inside. When the door opened, Phyllis regarded them warily. She'd stuck her blond hair atop her head, carelessly fastened with a pin, and her makeup looked smeared. Had she been crying, or had she simply dressed in a hurry?

"Come on in." She gave her sister a hug and then, over Bailey's shoulder, shot a what-the-hell look at Owen. "Is everything all right?"

"I'm fine." Bailey led the way inside. "Where's a good place to talk?"

Phyllis guided them through the entryway, down a hall and into a formal living room worthy of a Greek tycoon. As he took a seat on a striped, silk-covered Regency chair, Owen glanced at the closest niche and wondered who had picked out the bare-chested statue of a goddess with grape leaves in her hair.

He scarcely refrained from smacking himself in the forehead. This entire house screamed "expensive rental." Expensive and in questionable taste.

"We, uh…" Bailey cleared her throat. "I'm not complaining, but I missed my three-month checkup because I couldn't pay the doctor."

Phyllis remained standing by the fireplace, her fingers drumming lightly on the mantel. "Why not? We've given you a free place to live."

Arguing over finances was a waste of time. "The point is, I just administered an ultrasound," Owen said. "She's having twins."

He tried to sort out the expressions that flashed across Phyllis's face. Childlike amazement…concern…and a lot of other things that went by too fast to register. "So this is good news. Is it a boy and a girl?"

"Too soon to tell." Bailey sat forward on the edge of the sofa. "But they're unbelievable!" From her large purse, she produced a folder with a sonogram image Owen had given her.

Crossing the room, Phyllis studied it with a frown. "What's this?" Stepping away to avoid Bailey's attempt to help, she turned the picture. "Oh, I see. That's an arm, and...the head seems big. Is there something wrong with it?"

"They're completely normal, as far as I can tell," Owen assured her.

"Having twins is going to require more medical care," Bailey put in. "I can't keep fronting the money."

"Also, by the third trimester, she might need to take leave from work," Owen added. "Driving back and forth to a doctor in L.A. may be more than she can manage. Have you considered how you're going to take care of her?"

"One thing at a time." Phyllis sat down next to Bailey. "That's months away. You're fine for the moment, aren't you?"

"I feel great," Bailey said.

"And now that you've had this ultrasound, you can skip a checkup, which saves money," her sister put in. "By next month, we'll be in shape to afford anything you need. So what's the rush?"

"I... Maybe there isn't one."

Owen couldn't believe Bailey was buying this. "Having an informal sonogram does *not* substitute for a regular doctor visit. With twins, it'll be more necessary than ever to monitor her blood pressure and glucose level, among other things. Complications of pregnancy can come on suddenly and they can be life-threatening if not detected early."

"You just said they come on suddenly." Phyllis's glare

radiated darts in his direction. "If that's the case, how can they be detected early?"

"She's got you there," Bailey told him with a twist of a smile.

"This isn't a joke." Owen couldn't believe these two were dismissing his medical opinion. As if a nurse and her sister knew more than an expert in the field! "You require continuity of care. Do I need to explain that? Someone has to watch how you're changing and how the babies are growing."

"You promised you'd let me take the lead," Bailey burst out. "You're just along for the ride. And maybe to offer a little medical advice, which we're free to accept or not."

"This isn't your baby—aren't your babies," Phyllis amended. It was an open challenge, as if she were daring him to speak up.

Owen nearly took the bait. But what then? If he claimed paternity, that wouldn't change the fact that he'd agreed to father a baby for his brother. In every state that he was aware of, a sperm donor gave up all rights to the offspring so long as the donation was freely made, the donor wasn't the woman's husband, and the insemination was performed by a licensed doctor. In this case, all three conditions had been met.

Most likely, the revelation would make Bailey angry enough to move out, and maybe in with Ned Norwalk or some other loopy friend of hers. The last thing he intended was to force her into an unstable living situation.

Worse, Owen would be shut out. Unable to watch the babies grow, and in no position to intervene if Bailey required it.

He swallowed his anger. "Since she's only three months along and seems healthy, the situation isn't critical. But by next month—"

"By next month, we'll be able to prepay those doctors for the entire maternity package." Phyllis bounced to her feet. "Which we'd intended to do, but some of our money got tied up offshore. These things happen. You do trust me, don't you, Bailey?"

Even as he saw the answering nod, Owen felt an unpleasant quiver of recognition. *Don't you trust me?* He'd heard Boone's father use that phrase during a visit while promising to return two weeks later. If memory served, the man had then disappeared for the better part of a year.

"Of course I do." Bailey jumped up and caught her sister's hands. "Isn't this fantastic? Boone will be thrilled, don't you think?"

Phyllis propped the ultrasound picture on the mantel, a precarious perch given the flexibility of the paper. "We're going to spoil those little darlings to death. You can help me decorate the nursery. Bears and dolls and books and the best furniture. Everything we dreamed about when we were growing up. Once we get this deal nailed down, we'll be rolling in it."

Rolling in what, exactly? Owen was tempted to ask. But Bailey clearly didn't share his skepticism.

"I'm so glad I can do this for you," she told her sister. "I love you, Phyllis."

"I love you too, honey." The blonde, a good three inches taller than Bailey, swept the younger woman into a fierce hug. Owen could have sworn there were tears in Phyllis's eyes. "Oh, wait! I have a present for you." She slipped out of the room and returned with a basket tied with a large bow. Inside he glimpsed bars of scented soap, bubble bath and other toiletries, along with a first aid kit. "Just a few things to help make you comfortable."

"They smell divine!" Bailey beamed at her.

These two shared a closer bond than he did with Boone,

Owen realized. While Phyllis might be guilty of magical thinking, assuming that problems would somehow resolve themselves, he didn't believe she would deliberately take advantage of her sister.

On the other hand, he was a lot less certain about his brother's motives toward anyone.

As he walked Bailey out through the foyer, Owen tried to imagine the twins racing about this elegant house, but he doubted that his brother would be able to keep the place. For most people, an ordinary house or a modest apartment would be fine, but Boone was never satisfied with ordinary. Otherwise, why spend a fortune renting a mansion when he couldn't afford doctor bills?

Owen shuddered to think how his brother would react if everything blew up in his face. Would Boone put his family first? And, if so, did that include the twins or were they simply another acquisition to him?

Today's visit had reinforced Owen's doubts. Boone's absence combined with Phyllis's initially tearful appearance, plus her grandiose claims that they would soon be rolling in money, all added up to much more than a question mark.

Owen conceded an obligation to keep his hands off Bailey's medical situation for the moment. But he had a moral obligation to protect her and the babies, as well as Boone's investors, from a shady setup.

Much as the prospect troubled him, it was time to pay a discreet visit to the police department's fraud unit. He hoped the authorities would be equally circumspect in making sure they got all the facts before this matter spun out of control.

Chapter Eight

The following week, Bailey had only passing encounters with Owen at breakfast and late at night, and occasionally at the medical center. But she felt his presence everywhere.

Sunday night, he left his underwear in the dryer and she had to remove it in order to dry her own stuff, which seemed rather rude. But fascinating, too. The man wore black jockeys, very sexy.

At work on Wednesday, she heard he'd lost his temper at his new office nurse, Keely Randolph, a heavyset woman who refused to indulge the doctor's preferences regarding office procedure. While Keely might not be the most popular individual at Safe Harbor Med, much of the nursing staff was rooting for her. No one else had wanted to take on the pugnacious Dr. T. after his previous nurse left.

Bailey relished the fact that Keely was unimpressed by hotshot surgeons. As for Ned, he'd begun taking bets on how long Keely would last, with additional points for guessing whether she'd transfer to another office first or be sent packing. It was all in fun, with most of the money to go to charity. The winner would receive a gift certificate to the hospital cafeteria.

But although she enjoyed listening to the chatter at lunchtime, Bailey wished her friends wouldn't keep prodding her to reveal details of Owen's behavior at home.

"He's entitled to *some* privacy," she said on Thursday to Devina Gupta, a nurse who worked for pediatrician Samantha Forrest, and Lori Ross, who was Dr. Rayburn's nurse as well as the wife of a neonatologist.

At an adjacent table, she caught a slight nod from newcomer Erica Benford, who tended to sit by herself or with other surgical nurses. Obviously, Erica approved of Bailey's discretion, but then, she had a well-known loyalty to Owen, since they'd worked together for years.

Bailey wished Erica would join them, because there was a lot she wanted to know. She'd heard from Patty and Alec that Owen had appeared at social events in Boston with several stunning women, often with credentials that rivaled his own. Not that she would dare to ask directly, but had there been anyone special, anyone who might reappear without warning?

"It's just strange that you two are related by marriage," said Devina, lifting a glass of orange juice carefully with her beautifully manicured fingers. None of the other nurses could figure out how she kept her nails that perfect, and Devina never revealed her secret.

"He's not so bad," Bailey said. *Especially when he runs his hands over my abdomen.* His touch still tingled through her, and she got warm every time she recalled him staring at the screen, fascinated by the babies' antics in the womb.

Why was he so protective about her medical care? He'd insisted on going with her to see Phyllis and, although she would never admit it, she'd been touched by the way he'd stood up for her

Don't start thinking you matter to him. It was a crazy idea, for all kinds of reasons. Also, a great way to get her heart bruised and end up feeling like a fool.

"You're defending him? Unbelievable." Ned made up

the fourth person at their table. "Are you going to eat that roll? If not, I'll take it."

Devina pretended to slap his hand. "Don't be greedy. She's eating for two."

"Or more," Lori said. "Are you sure your doctor didn't detect anything?"

Since Bailey normally revealed whatever was on her mind, she nearly answered with the truth. But how could she explain suddenly knowing that she carried twins, when she'd been telling everyone that nothing had showed up at her last exam?

"I'd better get back to work." She handed the roll to Ned. "Enjoy."

"Are you avoiding the subject?" Devina challenged.

"Dr. Franco's going to Hawaii next week and I've got a lot to do," Bailey reminded her. August had arrived, and with it Nora's delayed honeymoon. "We're squeezing in as many patients as possible."

"Thanks." Ned began buttering the roll. "By the way, I'm trying to firm up my weekend plans, seeing as I'm such a popular guy. How about if I drop by on Saturday?"

Usually, she enjoyed singing together, ordering pizza and watching old movies. Having Ned around seemed to irk Owen, which was also a definite plus. But Bailey didn't feel like hanging with her buddy Saturday night. "I'm counseling in the afternoon and it might run late." Renée had called to request a three o'clock get-together. Maybe they'd have coffee afterward, although Bailey had pretty much lost her taste for the brew. "Another time."

"No problem."

She sensed her friends watching as she wove her way between crowded tables. Even from across the large room, Bailey recognized their voices as the conversation resumed. Although she couldn't make out any words, she had a pretty good idea that they were talking about her and her newfound reluctance to spill all.

She didn't entirely understand it herself. It wasn't only because of her sometimes confusing feelings about Owen, either.

Instinctively, Bailey's hand closed over her midsection as she walked next door to the medical office building. Inside, still too small for her to detect their movements, lay her children.

No, Phyllis's children, and Boone's. A deal was a deal. But instead of focusing on proper diet and when to start childbirth classes, her brain kept returning to two little individuals. Boys? Girls? What names would Phyllis choose? Surely she'd let Bailey babysit—probably insist on it.

What if they moved away? Bailey's throat tightened at the idea. The kids might grow up as virtual strangers, yet she had no right to insist that they stay here in Safe Harbor forever. What if they came back to her years later, armed with the truth, and demanded to know why she'd given them up?

She couldn't talk about this with her friends. There'd be a smattering of I-warned-you's, and all sorts of opinions about how and what she should do. But to them, it would be nothing more than idle chitchat. To Bailey, this meant more with every passing day.

Because with each new day, her children were growing. That meant the moment was approaching when she'd have to hand them over to someone else.

As for Owen, he seemed to have forgotten all that caring uncle stuff. On Thursday, he arrived home late, grabbed a sandwich and got busy checking his email, or whatever he did on his computer. Bailey missed the way they'd joked together in the hot tub and during the ultrasound. She even tried to pick an argument by removing his laundry from the dryer while it was still damp and leaving it on the couch, but if he noticed, he ignored it.

On Friday, Bailey heard that he'd blown up at Keely for forgetting to ask a patient about current medications. Since prescription information was kept in the computer system, that was largely a formality for regular patients, but it could still be important. When Keely protested that she'd been interrupted twice, Owen had made a sarcastic rejoinder and the nurse had stalked out after calling him a string of adjectives in which *arrogant* and *egotistical* featured prominently.

That night, he hadn't come home by the time Bailey went to bed. She was just as glad. Poking a sleeping tiger might be amusing, but confronting one in full slasher mode would be unwise.

Saturday morning, he ate two of her yogurts and left money on the kitchen table to pay for them. What did he think she was, his housekeeper? Bailey grumbled silently when she found it. Fortunately she'd planned a foray to the supermarket anyway.

Since Nora had left and she had a slow week ahead, Bailey had expected to enjoy her free time. Instead, she was too restless to stroll through the mall and uneasy about calling any of her friends or her sister. Oddly, she missed Owen. Who else could she talk to about the twins?

She headed for the counseling center early, and spent half an hour chatting with the volunteer director, Eleanor Wycliff, about fundraising ideas. Promptly at three, Renée arrived. Although her hair remained an unflattering gray-brown, it seemed to Bailey that her eyes had more spark and she held her shoulders straighter.

They went into the counseling room, where Bailey sat on the frayed love seat while Renée took a folding chair.

Aside from a few more chairs, the only other furniture was a child's table with paper and markers set out.

"How's your week been?" Bailey asked.

"Thanks to you, I had an epiphany," Renée announced with a smile.

An epiphany? What did that mean exactly? Bailey recalled a church holiday, but she doubted that was what Renée meant. "Oh?"

"I decided to try on wigs to help me choose a color and style," the older woman said, smoothing down a pocket flap on her cargo pants. They were a lot more interesting than the outdated polyester ones she'd worn a week ago, Bailey mused.

"Good idea," she prompted.

"I walked into this wig and hat shop. There were two other women there and it took me about thirty seconds to realize they were both cancer patients." Renée paused a moment. "Here I am fretting about lacking a purpose in life, and these women are fighting to survive. To them, a wig didn't mean a new hairstyle, it meant a way to feel normal while undergoing chemotherapy."

"That was quite a revelation." Bailey hadn't expected Renée to have such an emotional experience over a simple change in hair color.

"As I said, I had an epiphany. It put my whole life into perspective. That's what I wanted to ask you about." Renée leaned forward, purpose blazing in her face.

Bailey had a sudden urge to run and fetch Eleanor, who was a lot older and more experienced. "I don't know much about putting life in perspective," she admitted. "I'm kind of confused about mine at the moment."

"Oh, not that!" The older woman chuckled. "I meant about volunteering at the hospital. They do use volunteers, don't they?"

"Absolutely." Relieved, Bailey gave her the name of the auxiliary coordinator who did the training and scheduling. "You could work in the gift shop or reception desk, assist visitors, take flowers and gifts to patients. Stuff like that. Our volunteers make everyone's life easier."

"I'd like to do that." Renée nodded vigorously. "I'm going to sign up next week. You've given me a future worth looking forward to, Bailey."

"Wow." That was unexpected. She didn't feel as if she deserved credit, but there was another area in which she might be able to help. "What about finding your son? I have a friend who's a detective. I could ask Patty to make inquiries."

Renée didn't hesitate. "No, thanks. Since my epiphany, I've decided to quit being so selfish. If my son wishes to find me, I've posted enough information to make that easy. If he doesn't, I'd only be intruding."

"Do you think kids have some special psychic connection to their birth parent?" Bailey asked. "I've been wondering about my own situation."

The other woman considered for a moment. "Emotionally, whether we feel a bond depends on our personality and maybe the family we grew up in. Your baby is going to be raised by relatives, so he or she won't be left guessing about where he came from. But I suspect everybody's different."

"Thanks." Although it was ironic that her client was counseling *her*, Bailey appreciated it. "You might want to sign up as a peer counselor here at the center, too. You have a natural talent."

"One new enterprise at a time. But I'll keep that in mind for later."

Happy to see Renée embark on a new course, Bailey

shook hands with her. "This isn't goodbye. I'm sure I'll see you around the medical center."

"We could have lunch occasionally," Renée suggested.

"That would be great!"

On the way home, Bailey picked up a double serving of Greek food—stuffed grape leaves along with moussaka, a baked eggplant dish. While she told herself she'd enjoy the leftovers, the truth was that she hoped she'd find someone at home to share it with.

But the driveway and the house were empty. Figuring Ned must be booked by now, and reluctant to invite him over when Owen was likely to be home soon, she ordered a new romance novel on her ebook reader. Then she settled down to eat and fall in love by proxy.

"I DON'T SEE HOW WE'RE EVER going to work this out," Alec Denny told Owen as they regarded the rows of incubators stacked like small refrigerators along a freshly painted wall.

"What seems to be the problem?" Owen asked in surprise. So far, their review of the new laboratories in the hospital's converted basement had been highly satisfactory. Alec had done a superb job of overseeing the remodeling and installation of sensitive equipment to process and preserve eggs, embryos and sperm.

"Patty wants to elope on a motorcycle, or possibly a skateboard. My daughter wants a big wedding where she can be the flower girl, and my mother thinks we should have a simple ceremony at her church." Alec stared toward a stereo microscope, but he wasn't really seeing it, Owen could tell.

Thank goodness there wasn't a problem with the labs. And for all his friend's joking complaints, the wedding plans didn't seem like much of a problem, either.

In the four years that he'd worked with the embryologist, he'd watched Alec weather a painful divorce from an unstable woman, win a custody battle and become a successful single dad. In all that time, Owen had never seen his friend glow with pure happiness until he fell back in love with his high school sweetheart.

"What kind of ceremony do *you* want?" he asked.

"I just want to marry Patty. We could do it on the back of a donkey for all I care."

"How romantic."

His friend shot him a puzzled glance. "Was that sarcasm? I never figured you'd care about things like that."

Neither had Owen. "It seems to me that if you're going to spend the rest of your life with a woman, the ceremony ought to be memorable."

"You don't think getting married on a donkey would be memorable?"

Owen burst out laughing. "Good point."

They finished their informal tour and made their way back along the corridor. It was nearly seven o'clock on Saturday night, and Owen reflected guiltily that he'd presumed on his associate's family time. "Go home. Take the rest of the weekend off."

"Will do." Jauntily, Alec led the way to the elevators. If he'd had any more bounce to his step, he'd have been skipping.

Even-tempered Alec was a good balance to Owen's razor-edged personality. More than once, the embryologist had served as a buffer with other staff members in Boston. He was tops in his profession, too. On the rare occasions that Alec put his foot down, whether about a medical matter or anything else, Owen had learned to back off.

He couldn't say the same for Keely Randolph. On the

drive home, it was hard to keep his foot off the accelerator as he replayed that ugly confrontation at the office. Granted, Owen shouldn't have dressed down the nurse in front of other staff members. Still, her neglect in updating a patient history could have had serious consequences. He'd discovered only through the patient's casual remark that she was taking an herbal supplement that could cause dangerous side effects in combination with her prescription medication.

He hadn't expected Keely to go storming off, but nursing supervisor Betsy Raditch had promised to find a temporary substitute by next week. Adjusting to yet another nurse wasn't going to be pleasant, but it should give him time to select someone who would suit him in the long term.

Approaching his house, Owen felt a spurt of pleasure at seeing a familiar car in the driveway. And no sign of any visitors.

Of course, Bailey might be in a crabby mood about those yogurts he'd pilfered this morning, even if he had paid for them. Halting at the curb, he wondered if he should swing by the supermarket and pick up a bouquet of flowers. Wasn't that what guys did to smooth things over?

Oh, for heaven's sake. He was overthinking this.

Grabbing his briefcase, he made his way up the walk. In the fading light, the overgrown tropical plants reminded him of the mysterious island of Bali Ha'i from Rodgers and Hammerstein's *South Pacific.* Or perhaps it was the song drifting from the front room in a lovely, clear alto that had put him in mind of his favorite composer and lyricist, even though it came from a different musical.

"When I Marry Mr. Snow" was from *Carousel.* Owen had fond memories of that musical from high school, when he'd played a major role. Lingering on the porch, he waited for another voice to join Bailey's, but none did. Thank goodness.

As she launched into a reprise, an impulse seized him. Without pausing to reflect, Owen opened the door, stepped inside and added his voice to hers.

Chapter Nine

In high school, Bailey used to fantasize about trying out for a musical, but she'd never had the nerve. Although her friends assured her that she had a great voice, she'd been afraid to call attention to herself. Her mother, who never stayed in one place for long, had moved out of the school district right before senior year, and Bailey had lied about her legal residence in order to remain with her friends.

She used to imagine herself center stage, launching into a song, when out of the wings stepped the handsome hero—or a boy who could pass for one with the right makeup and lighting—to join in the duet. Now, hearing a mellow, tuneful baritone and seeing Owen's teasing smile, she wondered if she'd fallen asleep at the keyboard. Any minute she might wake up.

Just keep singing and maybe this will last.

He barely took his gaze from hers as he crossed the living room, discarding his briefcase and sports coat on the couch, and skirted the dining table to join her. As he scooted into a chair beside her, Bailey reached the end of the song. Almost afraid to breathe, she flipped through the sheet music to the next song that caught her eye—"Shall We Dance?" from *The King and I.*

Not the wisest choice, considering that the lyrics spoke of dancing in each other's arms and lingering together, but she couldn't think straight with Owen's legs stretching against hers and his gaze fixed on her face. If she turned her head, they'd be practically nose to nose.

Or mouth to mouth.

Of their own accord, Bailey's fingers slid into the waltz tempo. A moment later, their voices blended so naturally that she couldn't remember why she'd hesitated.

This close, his heat enveloped her, and his voice reverberated into her nervous system. Instinctively, she swayed against him, and it seemed only natural when his arm wrapped around her waist. They might as well have been dancing.

After the last note faded, Bailey sat in silence, afraid to move. Owen's strength, his unexpected playfulness—everything about him—was larger than life. The other men she'd known had been boys compared with him.

"More," he murmured into her ear.

Bailey tried to clear her throat. "Any particular...?" She made the mistake of returning his gaze, only to find his mouth inches away.

His lips brushed hers, so lightly it was closer to a whisper than a kiss. "More," he repeated, but this time the word seemed to have a different meaning.

Bailey drew back. "Bad idea."

"Rough week?" Owen asked mildly.

"Not nearly as rough as yours."

He chuckled. "You heard about that, I take it."

"We had a bet going." Maybe she shouldn't have confided that, but what the heck?

"A bet?" The arch of his russet eyebrow conveyed a world of perplexity.

"I won a five-dollar gift certificate to the cafeteria." She'd split the grand prize with two other nurses.

"What did you bet on, precisely?" Owen asked.

"On who would cave first," she said.

He tilted his head, considering the implications. "You figured I'd hang tough?"

"Yep."

"Thanks for the vote of confidence."

"I'm not sure that's the right term," Bailey said.

"I didn't intend to sack Keely, even though she's been a thorn in my side. She's a competent nurse, despite some mistakes, but her attitude is unacceptable. If people don't admit fault and learn from their errors, they're likely to repeat them."

Bailey conceded the point. On the other hand, everyone knew that Owen vented his bad temper on whoever was around, the way he'd done with Ned, even without provocation. Thank goodness she didn't have to work for him.

Reaching around her, Owen riffled the pages of the music book. "Where'd you learn to play?"

Her family hadn't been able to afford formal piano lessons, which Bailey would have loved, but she'd been grateful for any instruction she could get. "One of my mom's boyfriends taught me a few things. He was a musician."

"A good one?"

"When he wasn't high as a kite."

"Ah." He gave no sign of removing his arm.

It had been a long day, Bailey reflected, resting her cheek on his shoulder. It was just the right height. "You'd make some woman a terrific pillow," she murmured before realizing how suggestive that sounded. "I didn't mean that!"

She felt his rumble of laughter. "I like the way you speak without thinking. It's refreshing."

"It's awkward." She doubted those elegant women he'd dated in Boston were so unguarded.

He reached down to touch her stomach. "The twins are growing fast. Do they ever ask about me?"

"I heard them complaining a while ago," Bailey answered tartly, adding in a high voice, "'Where's that doctor who poked and prodded us? Punch him out for us, will you, Mom?'"

"Is that an exact quote?" His palm cupped the bulge, while his thumb performed a gentle, circular massage.

Did he have any clue about the sensations rippling through her? Perhaps, but he was joking around, nothing more. Maybe having a bit of fun at her expense. The notion stiffened Bailey's resistance, until curiosity got the better of her. "They aren't growing too fast, are they?"

"No. It's simply more noticeable because there are two of them." He leaned back, releasing her from the heated cocoon they'd shared. "Any word from your sister?"

She hadn't heard a thing from Phyllis, a fact that added to Bailey's irritation. "Quit nagging!"

He blinked with an air of innocence, except that no one would credit the great Dr. T. with any such thing. "It was a friendly inquiry."

"You don't trust her!"

"I don't trust my brother." He paused as if considering whether to say more.

Bailey didn't care to hear it. Several times this week, she'd awakened in a panic with visions of her nest egg gone forever and the twins disappearing with her sister and brother-in-law along an endless road toward the horizon. But since there was nothing she could do about the situation, why waste time worrying? "Some of us have a sense of family loyalty."

"Some of us know our siblings better than we wish we did." There was regret in his words. "Enough gloom and doom. Feel like a dip in the hot tub?"

Bailey's breasts tightened at the prospect of heated water rippling between them. The impact of his kiss lingered, along with the emotional imprint of his hand on her abdomen. Her pregnancy wasn't too far advanced for lovemaking, and her body felt ripe for pleasure.

He was watching her, his expression keen with anticipation. Judging by the way he'd caressed her a moment ago, he was probably a skilled lover who knew exactly how to arouse a woman. A few minutes of nearly naked cuddling in the hot tub and she'd pass the point of no return.

What she needed was a real boyfriend, not a hit-and-run guy taking advantage of the moment. While Owen might not be deliberately treating her as an easy mark, that's what she'd be. *I'm not his type and he...* Well, he wasn't hers, although she'd never actually encountered his type before. "I'm tired. Past my bedtime."

"It's eight o'clock."

"I'm sleeping for three," she responded.

From the shadow in his eyes, she half expected him to try to dissuade her, but he merely closed the book of sheet music and pushed back his chair. "Then I'd better fix myself some dinner."

"I went to the grocery store," she said, as if that wouldn't be obvious when he opened the fridge. "That is *not* an invitation to help yourself. This house doesn't come with a personal shopper."

"Don't worry. When you get too big to roll your way through the supermarket aisles, you can hand me a list and I'll do the honors." Off he went to the kitchen, as casually as if he hadn't proposed a steamy encounter in the hot tub, and as if her refusal didn't mean a thing.

Had she misunderstood his intentions? Bailey switched off the keyboard and covered the keys. This living arrangement was way too convenient for a man like Owen, who was obviously accustomed to getting his way. And dangerous to a woman like her, who tended to leap before she looked.

Not this time. Tomorrow, she planned to attend a jazz concert with friends in the afternoon, followed by dinner and a movie. As for next week, with any luck, Owen would be tied up with his usual nonstop schedule, and when he came home, she'd retreat to her room or have guests over.

One way or another, Bailey intended to keep distance between them until Owen found a woman of his type. Then, she felt certain, he'd forget all about her.

How did you protect a woman who resolutely refused to believe a word against her sister? Owen wasn't sure exactly how he meant to protect her. Whatever money she'd invested couldn't be instantly retrieved, and as for the babies...

Sitting in the kitchen finishing a frozen dinner that was more sauce than meat and potatoes, Owen basked in his awareness of those precious children. Moments ago, with his palm only inches from their tiny selves, he'd experienced a flood of love that left him weak. He'd never known such a powerful desire to cherish and guard anyone or anything. It surpassed reason and logic.

Nor had he figured out how to separate his bond with the babies from his connection to Bailey. Normally, he dated women who kept their emotions under lock and key, and allowed him to do the same. They enjoyed each other for a while, kept company, shared social and professional insights, and parted when the relationship became inconvenient or threatened to dissolve into petty arguments.

Amazingly, he enjoyed arguing with Bailey. Not only

could she hold her own, but she skewered him in unpredictable ways. She never pulled her punches out of respect for his temper, either. He'd begun to suspect that she deliberately provoked him. It had been fun ignoring the damp laundry on the couch and noting her disappointment.

As he discarded his empty plastic container and put his glass in the dishwasher, Owen was keenly aware of the noises from Bailey's bedroom. The walls were thin enough for him to hear the scrape of a drawer, followed by a faint rustling. Was she putting on one of those silly T-shirts she slept in? Any minute, she'd tromp into the bathroom and splash water all over the counter as she brushed her teeth. Was she going to pull another trick? He'd bought a couple of extra toothbrushes, just in case she decided to hide his old one.

He caught himself grinning as he tried to figure out how he could get back at her. This was childish. Beneath him. But a terrific stress reliever after intense days of building up to the program's opening next month.

Speaking of which, he had a little more work to get done tonight. At the dining room table, now bare of the keyboard, Owen set up his laptop and forced his attention on his email. Dispatching new messages at night cleared valuable time in the morning.

Most of the items were routine, but partway down his in-box he found excellent news. Jan Rios Garcia, an administrative nurse he'd worked with a few years earlier, had accepted the job of coordinator for the planned egg donor program at Safe Harbor. That was one of the key posts Owen had been concerned about filling. He responded enthusiastically.

He loved being surrounded by capable, trustworthy colleagues. If only he could find a suitable replacement for his office nurse, he'd be in great shape.

Before logging off, Owen ran a search under his brother's name. The only thing that turned up was a discreet website for Boone's investment company. Nothing screamed *Scam!*—no promises of outrageous returns, no glossy pictures of the resort development depicted in Boone's office. But then, his brother was too smart to reveal himself on the internet. From what Owen recalled, the senior Mr. Storey had pitched his projects in person to small groups and individuals.

During his lunch break on Wednesday, Owen had visited the police station and spoken with a Detective Hank Driver in the fraud unit. The man made notes and asked questions that quickly took on a sharp edge. To Owen's annoyance, he got the impression the detective was trying to figure out whether Owen had an ulterior motive or some personal involvement in his brother's business. He'd been on the verge of walking out angrily when Leo Franco, Nora's husband, stepped into the interview room and greeted him in friendly fashion.

That put an end to the inquisition, but left him deeply unsatisfied. If doubting the motives of a reporting party was Detective Driver's idea of investigating, nothing was likely to be accomplished.

His suspicions might be off base, Owen reminded himself. He hated the idea of betraying his brother. It would be a relief if Boone was cleared.

From Bailey's room came the sound of the TV. Since she didn't usually keep the set turned on as background noise, he gathered she'd decided to watch a program. A sitcom, judging by the laugh track.

She hadn't been tired. She was avoiding him.

As he leaned his elbows on the table, an idea popped into his mind. It would help him out of a temporary bind, and irk Bailey at the same time. That struck him as a win-win situation.

Smiling to himself, he fired off an email to the hospital's nursing coordinator.

ON MONDAY MORNING, BAILEY had the rare luxury of doing follow-ups on some patients at Nora's request. She started with Una Barker, a former fertility patient who, after two years of trying to conceive, had recently adopted a baby. Una and her husband had avoided advanced fertility treatments because of the cost.

"Our son is adorable!" Una crowed on the phone. "I keep meaning to bring him by the office like Dr. Franco asked, but I've been busy."

"I can imagine. Don't forget your regular checkup." Bailey consulted her computer. "You're due in a couple of months. Do you want to make that appointment now?"

"Sure."

After they finished, she made a note for Nora when she returned from her honeymoon, then followed up with Lucy Arrigo. She and her husband objected to in vitro fertilization on religious grounds, and when less aggressive methods failed to result in pregnancy, they also had adopted.

"I can't believe how happy I am, even though I'm exhausted, too," Lucy said. "Thanks so much for checking on me." She also scheduled her regular exam.

Nora would be happy to hear about Una and Lucy, Bailey reflected. Owen had cited their cases—anonymously, of course—as examples of how Nora's old-fashioned methods failed to produce results. But the choice belonged to the patients, not the doctor, and the adoptions had turned out well.

Bailey went to fix herself a cup of herbal tea. The receptionist was subbing in another office, and except for a few phone calls from patients, the place was quiet.

When the office door opened, she wasn't entirely surprised to see Betsy Raditch, the hospital's director of nursing. Although the doctors ran their own private practices, most of them contracted with the hospital to supervise the staffing arrangements.

"We have a request for you to fill in at another doctor's office this week." Betsy adjusted her glasses as she glanced at the clipboard in her hand.

"Dr. Sargent?" Bailey had more or less expected to be drafted to help the relatively new obstetrician, who'd agreed to take on any of Nora's cases that required immediate attention.

"Not him." Standing in the empty waiting room, Betsy shifted her stance. A straightforward woman in her forties, she seemed unusually tense. "It's, um, Dr. Tartikoff."

He wouldn't dare! "Excuse me?" Bailey said.

"I realize you two are housemates and, I gather, related by marriage, so this could be awkward." Betsy met her gaze at last. "But I have confidence in your professionalism."

Okay, Bailey mused, she had known that Owen lacked a nurse, but she'd never imagined he would have the nerve to request her. Yet she could hardly refuse. On what basis?

"Did Dr. Tartikoff make the request himself, or was it someone else's suggestion?" Perhaps a well-meaning third party such as the administrator had proposed this notion.

"Definitely him. He has great confidence in your abilities," Betsy assured her. "It's an honor. And with everything the hospital has invested in the opening, keeping things running smoothly for Dr. Tartikoff is of the highest priority."

What about keeping things running smoothly for me?
But she could hardly use that as an objection. Also, Bailey
supposed she did owe the guy a favor in return for performing the ultrasound.

"Okay," she heard herself say. "When do I start?"

The answer, as she'd feared, was, "Right now."

Chapter Ten

Starting work at a new doctor's office required time to adjust. While the overall job requirements were similar, countless small variations could trip you up, plus you needed to get up to speed on the day's patients.

As if that weren't bad enough, it was almost ten o'clock. While Owen—she'd better think of him as Dr. Tartikoff on the job, Bailey reflected grimly—had been in surgery earlier, there were already two patients in the waiting room. They should have been prepped by now.

The receptionist, Caroline Carter, a sweet young woman with a complexion like chocolate milk and swingy shoulder-length black hair, greeted her with a touch of apprehension. "We're expecting him any minute."

"Charts?" Bailey asked. "Schedule?"

Caroline provided them. Bailey revved to near light speed as she readied the examining rooms, determined the purpose of the patients' visits and set out gloves and other equipment for Owen. For *him*, as Caroline had put it. Thank goodness he was running late, because Bailey managed to get the first two women weighed, take their medical histories and leave them to change into hospital gowns before she heard the staff door open and male footsteps speed along the linoleum.

In the hallway, Owen loomed twice as large as usual.

Except for a blink as he registered Bailey's presence, he made no comment. Instead, he glanced irritably at the red lights outside the examining rooms. "What're they doing in there, trying on the gowns for size?"

Ignoring the remark, she handed him the first chart. "Mrs. Stanfield is here for her initial workup…"

After that, the morning sped by at an exhausting pace. Word of Owen's arrival had drawn eager patients from across the region, many of them driving several hours to consult with him. And Dr. T. allocated only a few hours a day to clinic visits, sandwiching them between surgery and administrative duties.

Yet, Bailey noted when she assisted him at exams, he listened carefully to each woman's concerns and explained his observations and recommendations fully. Perhaps not with the same depth as Nora, but he did give his reasons along with brochures and addresses of websites that could fill in more details.

By two-thirty, when the last patient departed in a state of near-bliss at having seen the great doctor, Bailey could have given the spiel herself. In vitro fertilization—IVF—involved harvesting eggs from the woman, fertilizing them with sperm in a lab, and implanting them in the woman's womb. Test tube babies, once a science fiction premise, had become routine. The procedure gave hope to women with a wide variety of problems, from blocked fallopian tubes to endometriosis and ovulation disorders.

But there was more, far more. She'd never even heard of intracytoplasmic sperm injection, for cases where the man's sperm count was very low. Under a microscope, a single sperm could be injected directly into an egg during IVF. That was, she gathered, embryologist Alec Denny's department.

Bailey was impressed at the wealth of options available

to these patients and their husbands. "It's amazing that I conceived so easily," she commented as Owen washed up after the last patient's departure. "Whatever else you might say about Boone, he's certainly potent."

She could have sworn he started to laugh. "Guess he must be. Hey, you want to grab lunch?"

Bailey stared at him in horror. "Are you kidding? If people see us eating together, there'll be no end to the gossip."

Owen shot her a look of frustration. "We eat dinner together occasionally. Big deal."

"They don't witness that." She supposed she shouldn't speak too freely, but working for Nora had put her in the habit of being frank with her doctor. "Why'd you request me?"

"Why not?" he countered.

"Better be careful. All those compliments will turn a girl's head."

Owen chuckled. "I hear you're a good nurse."

"That's more like it." Well, it was only for the week, she supposed. "See you around."

She felt his gaze following her as she collected her purse at the nurses' station and headed through the empty waiting room. Caroline stopped munching on her brown-bagged salad and peered at her wide-eyed. "He invited you to lunch?" She had sharp ears.

"I'm sure it won't happen again," Bailey told her.

"Yes, but—wow."

The man must have acted totally aloof until now. Bailey didn't have to stretch her imagination very far to imagine that.

She spent the afternoon returning phone calls for both Nora and Owen. There were always small problems to smooth over, as well as prescription refills that needed authorization and questions to answer. Some she could field herself, and others she referred to Owen or, in the case of Nora's patients, to Dr. Sargent.

Monday night, Owen returned home late and she heard him on the phone, snapping at Dr. Rayburn. Apparently the hospital corporation's offer hadn't been tempting enough to lure a world-renowned urologist whom Owen wanted to head the male fertility part of the program. While that was hardly Dr. Rayburn's fault, the affable administrator made an easier target than the hospital's owners two thousand miles away in Louisville, Kentucky.

On Tuesday, she discovered that the scheduling desk had failed to reach some patients to confirm appointments, so there were two no-shows and several late arrivals. Around eleven-thirty, to Bailey's dismay, the waiting room remained empty for fifteen minutes, and then four women arrived simultaneously.

She was taking the first patient's medical history when Owen peered angrily into the room. "Not ready?" he demanded.

"I'm sorry, Doctor," she said, keenly aware of the patient sitting right there. "We had a bit of confusion with the appointments."

Owen glared. "This is unacceptable."

"I agree, but…"

He stalked out. To her dismay, Bailey realized he must have grabbed the next chart, because she heard the door open to the waiting room and Owen's voice call out a patient's name.

Bailey felt her cheeks flame. "I'm just a substitute," she told the woman perched on the examining table.

The woman gave her a sympathetic smile. "Geniuses can be difficult."

Geniuses can be a royal pain in the butt. But all Bailey

could do was nod agreement and try not to skip anything important as she finished taking down information.

Despite—or perhaps because of—the doctor's meddling, it took a while to make up for lost time, since Bailey refused to sacrifice thoroughness to his impatience. Not only did Owen refuse to meet her gaze when they were in an examining room together, he also employed a sarcastic tone when speaking to her in front of patients. Didn't the man have any idea he was acting like a jerk?

By half past noon, when the last patient departed with lab paperwork in hand, Bailey wondered how Keely had lasted even a week. Thank goodness Dr. T. had no patients scheduled in the afternoon, because she required at least eighteen hours to recuperate.

Caroline stopped by the nurses' station. "Are you all right?"

"No!" Before Bailey could elaborate, she saw the door open from Owen's private office. She'd figured he would have flown the coop already, since he rarely stuck around five seconds longer than necessary.

His eyes—not cinnamon today, but fiery red peppers, or so they seemed to Bailey—skewered her. "I expected better from you, Nurse."

Caught out in the open, Caroline swallowed hard and took a tentative step backward.

"I expected better from *you*," Bailey replied tightly.

The receptionist turned and fled. Who could blame her?

"I beg your pardon?" Owen's jaw hung open in astonishment. Apparently he hadn't expected her to confront him and risk the full force of his fury.

"Are you aware that the scheduling desk was short-handed yesterday due to an illness and didn't confirm a lot of your appointments?" Bailey demanded. "They should have notified me to pick up the slack, but they got their

wires crossed and left a message on Keely's cell phone."
She'd had Caroline check out the source of the problem
earlier.

For a moment, the doctor didn't move. He just stood
there in his white coat, holding a folder and processing
the information. "I wasn't informed of that."

"I'm informing you now!" Bailey knew she ought to
simmer down, but with maternal hormones on the ram-
page, she lacked even the modest amount of self-control
she usually possessed.

"I suppose that does put a different light on things,"
Owen conceded.

"You embarrassed me in front of patients. Has it ever
occurred to you that nurses take pride in our professionalism? We aren't put here to be emotional punching bags for
your bad temper."

He inhaled, fast, a couple of times. "Point taken."

She stood there, arms folded, keenly aware that he
hadn't finished. She could almost see the thoughts tumbling around in his brain, like balls in a lottery basket.

What emerged, finally, was "I'm sorry."

"Apology accepted." She decided not to push her luck
by pointing out that he ought to be sorry. "I'll see you
tomorrow. Or...sooner."

"Very good." With a bob of the head, he was off at his
usual lightning pace.

Bailey gave herself a moment to recover. Had she really
just confronted the tyrant of Safe Harbor Medical Center
and come out unscathed? Whew.

She stuck her head into the reception area. There sat
Caroline, cell phone pressed to her ear, in the midst of
saying, "...apologized! Can you believe it?"

"Hang up," Bailey told her.

Alarm fleeted across the young woman's face. "Gotta go," she told her unseen friend, and clicked off.

"You are not to repeat anything you hear in this office," Bailey told her sternly. Caroline's stunned expression gave her pause, but right now she had to be Owen's nurse, not everybody's best friend. "Patients and doctors need to be able to trust that this is a safe, secure and private environment. If you want to stay in the medical profession, you need to learn to be discreet. I won't report you this time but don't let it happen again."

"I won't." The receptionist took a couple of rapid breaths. "I didn't think… I mean, everybody's been so interested…"

"And it made you feel important to be the source of information," Bailey finished. "I know it's tempting, but if Dr. Tartikoff had heard you, you might have been fired."

"I'll never do it again. I promise." Caroline sounded deeply earnest. "I'm really sorry."

Two apologies in the span of a few minutes had to be a record in Bailey's experience. "Just don't forget."

"I won't."

As she left, Bailey wished she could erase the guilt and unhappiness on the receptionist's face. She hated being an authority figure, but she hoped she'd handled this correctly. A stern warning now might save Caroline's career, as well as safeguard the entire office.

Next they'll be saying I've turned into a miniature version of Dr. T. Still, reprimands were sometimes necessary. The key was to show respect for the person on the receiving end.

In the cafeteria, a trio of interested faces greeted her as she approached with her tray. "You bearded the lion in his den and survived!" Devina said.

Oh, great. "Has everybody heard about that?" Bailey asked as she took a seat.

"Just those of us who're alive and breathing." Lori shook her head. As the wife of a physician, surely she understood the delicate issues involved. "Somebody's got a loose tongue."

"Not me, I assure you. And it's been taken care of," Bailey replied, unwilling to say anything further that might hurt Caroline.

Ned's teeth gleamed white against his surfing tan. "You took quite a risk, calling him on his rudeness."

"Didn't think I had it in me?" she teased.

"I didn't think he had it in *him*," Ned said. "It being humility. Erica's been telling us he's basically a good guy, but I'm not sure anybody believed her."

Bailey focused on cutting up her chicken and dumplings while she considered how to stem the flood of chatter. The best she could come up with was to provide a different item for folks to gab about. "By the way, did I mention that I'm expecting twins?"

"I knew it!" Lori crowed.

"Children are expensive to raise these days." Although she didn't look a day over thirty-five, Devina had a son in medical school. "But I suppose your sister and her husband can afford it."

Considering that as far as Bailey knew, they still hadn't paid her doctor, that might not be true. "I suppose so."

To her relief, the topic for the rest of the meal shifted to babies and other hospital news, including the hiring of a head for the planned egg donor program. "I hear Dr. Sargent's very interested in working with that project," Lori said.

"Terrific." But Bailey wasn't really listening. She was already planning ways to keep Owen's office running smoothly for the rest of the week, to emphasize her point about professionalism.

She'd demanded his respect. And she intended to earn it.

Chapter Eleven

Although Owen tried to turn a deaf ear to hospital undercurrents, he soon discovered that word of his blowup with Bailey had spread far and wide. He shouldn't have been surprised, knowing how open she was, but respect cut both ways. This matter should have been kept strictly between them.

Still, he couldn't muster up enough outrage to challenge her about it. For one thing, she proved an ideal nurse for the rest of the week, staying on top of developments, working skillfully with patients and anticipating his needs as a doctor. Too bad that, under the circumstances, he had zero chance of securing her in that position on a permanent basis.

Working as well as living with her, Owen had become keenly aware of the babies' day-by-day development. Normally, he only saw maternity patients once a month at this stage, and took the miraculous changes more or less for granted. But these were *his* children swelling her abdomen.

And then there was Bailey herself. Bailey who sang beautifully in the shower and left funny little notes in the refrigerator ("Hands off or you die!"). When she paused to put her feet up in the middle of the day, he felt concern rather than annoyance. When he saw her eating lunch with Ned, a wave of something akin to jealousy washed over him.

On Thursday, when he arrived home early enough to sing a couple of duets with her—they'd exhausted their favorites from Rodgers and Hammerstein and moved on to *My Fair Lady*—Owen nearly told her the truth about his paternity. He wasn't sure what good it would do, but she deserved to know, and besides, he held out the sneaking hope that she'd draw a little closer to him and a little farther from her pal Ned. But then he remembered how she'd spread word of his apology.

Most secrets caused only temporary embarrassment when they traveled through the hospital grapevine. If they reached the press, they ran off like raindrops on an airplane. But Owen feared that the news of his involvement in this soap opera surrogacy situation might cause a crash landing. So he kept it to himself.

On Friday morning, he spent a couple of hours in Dr. Rayburn's office with Jennifer Martin and, by videoconference from her office in Louisville, Chandra Yashimoto, the Medical Center Management vice-president. They reviewed plans for the opening the following month, including a series of press conferences, seminars and events for the public.

These would be followed, in October, by a meeting in Los Angeles of the International Society of Embryology and Reproductive Fertility, at which Owen was to be the keynote speaker. Alec Denny had also been tapped for a prestigious panel. One of the highlights would be a paper presented by Cole Ratigan, M.D., the specialist from Minneapolis whom Owen had sought to head his men's fertility program.

"The conference will give you two a chance to get better

acquainted," Chandra suggested. "Maybe you can change his mind. Otherwise we'll have to find someone else."

Owen ground his teeth. When he fixed his aim on a specialist, he hated having to settle for a second or third choice. "Surely the corporation can sweeten its offer."

"I took the liberty of calling him personally." Chandra, normally tough as nails, cleared her throat in what looked, on the computer screen, like embarrassment. "It seems that money isn't the issue."

"What is?" Mark Rayburn asked.

"He's concerned that there might be a clash of personalities."

That surprised Owen. "With me?"

"He gave that impression," the executive said.

Owen had never crossed swords with Cole that he could recall. In fact, their interaction at previous conferences had been pleasant. "I'm floored."

No one spoke.

"Okay, I can be hard to get along with," Owen conceded. "But only..." *Only for people who're working under me. Which Cole would be.* Was his reputation really that bad?

"Moving right along, who else do you have in mind?" Chandra asked.

He provided a couple of names. They wrapped up the videoconference by eleven-fifteen, which gave him a chance to drop by his hospital office down the hall from Mark's before heading to the medical building next door.

Hurrying into the outer office, Owen gave a start as a blond man jumped to his feet. What was Ned Norwalk doing here—planning to challenge him to a duel over Bailey? Well, she hadn't been singing duets with Ned lately, so he doubted the fellow had a chance. "Yes?"

"Nurse Norwalk asked to wait for you," the receptionist put in. "I hope that's all right."

Despite his irritation, Owen reminded himself that the man might have business of a nonpersonal nature. Besides, it was hardly fair to vent at the guy simply for the crime of eating lunch with Bailey. "Of course," he said. "Come in."

The nurse gave a quick nod and followed. Judging by his rapid breathing, he was nervous about something.

Growing more curious by the minute, Owen offered him a chair and then sat behind the desk. "What's on your mind?"

"I'd like to work for you." Ned swallowed as if about to say something further, then sat back and waited.

"I beg your pardon?" Owen took a moment to grasp the man's meaning. "You mean in my office?"

Ned nodded. The fellow was offering to take over as Owen's nurse. That was unexpected. "Mind if I ask why?"

"Even in high school, I liked taking care of people. I used to work summers as a lifeguard. At first, when I decided to become a nurse, my friends teased me, but I knew it was right for me." Ned spoke with a thoughtfulness Owen hadn't noticed before. Not that he'd paid much attention.

Owen had never worked closely with a male nurse. "That doesn't explain why you're seeking a transfer from surgery. That *is* what you're doing now, I believe."

"That's right, sir." Ned's steady manner was growing on Owen. "As I said, I like people. Listening to them. Making sure nothing gets overlooked. In surgery, I barely meet them before they're anesthetized. And when I work the recovery room, they're so groggy that mostly I'm just checking their vital signs."

"We're going to have a number of new physicians joining the staff," Owen said. "Why choose me? I'm a notorious pain in the neck."

Ned's mouth twisted wryly. "I have to admit, you did

snap at me without good cause, and everybody knows about your problems with Keely. Hope you don't mind my being candid."

"I don't." Owen preferred honesty to simmering resentment.

The younger man shrugged. "Erica speaks highly of you. According to the grapevine, Keely walked out—you didn't fire her, so I can't hold that against you. And there's a certain prestige in working for a doctor in your position."

Was the fellow seeking status? If so, it would come at a high cost. "Make sure you understand that I'm tough to work for. I have very high standards, and I don't make nice with people's feelings."

"But when Bailey called you on your behavior, you were gracious enough to apologize," Ned replied.

Owen's jaw tightened. "She shouldn't have discussed that with other staff members."

"She didn't." The nurse frowned. "I mean, only after someone else spoke about it first. I'm not sure who, to tell you the truth."

"Then how can you be sure it wasn't Bailey?"

"She was unhappy that we'd all heard about it." Ned seemed to be searching his memory. "She mentioned something about the leak having been taken care of. Then she clammed up, which is totally unlike Bailey. Or used to be."

That left only one other possibility as the source. Annoyed as Owen felt about the receptionist, she *was* young. He decided to get Bailey's input before taking any action, since she apparently believed she'd handled the problem.

In any event, he had a decision to make about Ned's request. Frankly, it struck Owen as a good idea. A male nurse might not be quite as easily wounded as some of the women he'd worked with, and besides, he liked the fellow's directness.

"How does a three-month trial sound?" he said. "As long as you do your best, I promise not to hold it against you if it doesn't work out. By then you should have your choice of new physicians."

Ned let out a long breath. "Thank you, sir." He got to his feet, as did Owen, and the two shook hands across the desk. "You won't be disappointed."

"I appreciate your honesty. In moderation."

And, Owen mused as the nurse sauntered out with a light step, *I also appreciate your telling me about Bailey.*

She hadn't shot off her mouth at his expense. That meant a lot.

BAILEY COULD HAVE SWORN Owen had been paying close attention to her midsection all week. He'd been unusually attentive to her physical needs, too—massaging her shoulders on Thursday after she finished playing the keyboard, and encouraging her to put her feet up when they had a break between patients at the office.

She supposed some men found pregnant women attractive, but she'd picked up enough of his background from Erica to know that his dating choices tended toward sophisticated, high-powered and definitely *un*-pregnant ladies. As for his being the uncle, he and Boone weren't exactly close, so why should he care?

That left the possibility that he liked her. Which was really strange, since she was about as far from his usual type as you could get. The whole thing puzzled her and, worse, she couldn't discuss it with anyone. Not Patty, who was engaged to Owen's colleague. Besides, she was caught up in the ongoing debate about her wedding plans. Not Nora, because, even had she been here, she could hardly be expected to sympathize with Bailey's feelings on the subject of Dr. Tartikoff.

Which were…which were…

That she got tingly when he touched her. That she dreamed about floating in the hot tub with a nearly naked Owen, helping him lift her wet T-shirt over her head. That she replayed those dreams while wide-awake and eating a peanut butter sandwich in the office on Friday.

Blame it on the pregnancy hormones. Blame it on the long drought in her love life. Blame it on chemistry.

Bailey used to wish that, once in her life, she could fall completely and deeply in love. She didn't expect the guy to stick around, and once or twice she'd thought that she *might* be on the verge of falling in love. But a few tears and a week or so of misery had dispelled all that.

Owen was different. Her feelings scared her. If something happened between them, it would inevitably end badly. He'd go on his way, aloof and in charge and the center of everyone's attention. As for Bailey's pathetic excuse for a heart, she could already feel it threatening to betray her.

Well, she'd better whip it into shape, she decided as she finished the sandwich, because here he came, wearing a bemused expression. With an inward sigh, she lowered her feet and brushed the crumbs off the counter of the nurses' station. Although they didn't schedule regular patient visits on Friday, Owen reserved time after lunch for those who needed follow-ups or last-minute consults, and the women should be arriving shortly.

"Couple of things," he said, stopping in front of the station.

With a paper napkin, Bailey took a surreptitious swipe at her mouth and then sneaked a glance at the resulting smear. Darn. Peanut butter *and* jelly. "Did I miss anything?"

"On your face? No." Owen cocked his head. "Where's Caroline?"

Since he'd never so much as pronounced the receptionist's name in Bailey's hearing before, this struck her as odd. "She should be here any minute. She was filling in at Dr. Forrest's office this morning."

"She was the one who blabbed about our little squabble on Tuesday, wasn't she?" he said.

Uh-oh. Since he'd never mentioned the subject, Bailey had hoped he wasn't aware of the grapevine chatter. "Yes. I reprimanded her. She seemed to understand she'd behaved unprofessionally. Who told you?"

"Process of elimination."

"The only person you could have eliminated was me," she said. "What took you so long, and if you were ticked about it, why didn't you say so?"

He started to laugh. "Isn't there a limit on how many questions you can ask in one sentence?"

"Not that I'm aware of."

The man was in a remarkably good humor. He should be crabby, considering that as of Monday he'd be without a nurse again. "Spill," she said.

"I just took on Ned Norwalk as my new nurse." A grin played around the corners of his mouth as he watched her.

"You what?" Ned would be furious. He might even quit. "Whose big idea was that?"

"Ned's," Owen said.

Bailey's jaw dropped. It irked her to see that Owen was enjoying her reaction, but she didn't think he was making this up. "And you agreed?"

"He strikes me as competent, and I think he can handle my occasional flare-ups without bursting into tears."

"If you're too rough on him, we'll mock you behind your back," Bailey warned.

Owen shrugged. "I expect nothing less. Listen, since it's our last day together, so to speak, stick around after the patients leave. I'll let Caroline go home early."

"And?"

"You're at sixteen weeks," he said. "Let's do another ultrasound. If the babies cooperate, we might be able to tell the sex."

No matter how dubious she felt about the prospect of being alone with him, the opportunity was too good to pass up. "You're on. And Owen?"

An eyebrow lifted questioningly.

"Thanks."

"My pleasure," he said.

Not entirely his pleasure, Bailey thought ruefully. Because no matter how hard her brain cried out to be careful, her body ached for the sensual pleasure of his touch as he shared a rare moment of closeness with her and whatever little people lay inside.

Chapter Twelve

Owen was well aware that he'd earned a reputation for being a wizard with unborn babies. Not just in helping women conceive and carry pregnancies, but in dealing with the little tykes themselves. No one understood exactly how it worked, but under his gentle pressure, babies in breech position turned around in time to be delivered safely and obeyed his delicate urging to wriggle the kinks out of umbilical cords. Not always, but often.

He had a theory. He attributed his success to Rodgers and Hammerstein.

Take the twins. They'd grown remarkably in the nearly two weeks since he'd last wanded them, but as their cute little images appeared on the sonogram screen, they were in the wrong position for him to check out their gender. "They could use some encouragement," he warned Bailey. "Do you mind?"

"Whatever." She was staring at the screen as if utterly absorbed, but that didn't account for her rapid breathing.

After seeing a handful of patients and then sending Caroline home early—without any mention of her indiscretion—Owen had checked Bailey's blood pressure and heartbeat. Nothing wrong there. "I'm going to sing. Any objections?"

"Only if you require accompaniment."

"Not necessary." He didn't sing for many patients. Some women lacked a sense of humor, and some husbands took things the wrong way. But once in a while the babies needed it.

Usually, he encouraged his patients to join him in song, so the baby could feel the vibrations. This time, instead, Owen bent close to Bailey's abdomen and began to croon the words to "If I Loved You." With one hand caressing the bulge, he could feel the babies' rhythms shift, become dreamy. And gradually, as he prodded them, they yielded and rearranged themselves.

Bailey released a sigh. He sensed her heart rate slowing also. How sweet she looked, lying there trustingly, her eyelids half-shut, lost in the moment. Owen nearly forgot the purpose of the sonogram, until he felt another ripple beneath his hand. The natives were getting restless again, the ultrasound showed.

"Okay, little one." He manipulated the probe until he could plainly see one baby's shape. "It's a boy! Hold still now, little guy." Making sure he had a good view, he saved a shot.

"Both boys?" Bailey asked.

"Don't know yet."

"If you take requests, I'd like to hear 'There Is Nothing Like a Dame,'" she said.

"You think that will help?" Releasing the pressure, Owen sought a different angle while his mind played over what he'd just learned. He was going to have a son. A little boy to tussle with, a young man who'd grow up to chart a worthwhile course through life, like his father.

Like Boone?

The thought jolted Owen. What had he done by donating sperm to his brother? *I trusted him to deserve a child, that's what.*

With every passing day, his doubts were growing. He'd heard nothing about his brother returning from that unexplained trip. And Bailey still wasn't receiving regular medical care.

This little boy might grow up with his father in jail. And an uncle who, he recalled with a twinge of unease, might have helped to put him there.

"What happened to the music?" Bailey prompted.

"Sorry." But before he could launch into another tune, Baby Boy's sister presented a clear anatomical image. As he preserved the shot, Owen said, "You got your wish."

"It's a girl?" She beamed. "Phyllis will be thrilled."

"Talked to her lately?" Owen removed the device.

"Not for a few days." She tensed as if ready to argue, but he busied himself cleaning up.

A girl. They were having a girl, too. Lively and vulnerable like her mother. Owen averted his face to hide the flush of emotions.

He and Bailey ought to be picking out names and making plans. These were *their* kids, no doubt endowed with musical talents and a sense of humor and…

You can't keep them. Don't even think about that. What would he do with kids? Also, the very idea of him and Bailey trying to make a go of a family was preposterous. They couldn't even share a bathroom without squabbling.

He helped her sit up and wipe off the gel. "You feeling okay?"

"Why shouldn't I?"

"You've been awfully quiet." Normally, Owen would take his leave from a patient at this point. Instead, he slid his arms around Bailey and eased her down from the examining table. Round and solid, she smelled like a whole meadow full of beauty products.

"Don't you have to rush off somewhere?" She stood close against him in the flimsy gown.

He had emails to return, reports to read, decisions to make. "Not particularly. Want to grab a bite to eat?"

"Kind of early." The wall clock indicated a little past four.

"I never took you for a slave to convention." He brushed his cheek, bristly with end-of-day stubble, across the top of her head.

"Are we going to play nurse and doctor?" she asked.

"Okay." He grinned at the notion.

"Which one do you want to be?"

The man who takes you home and keeps you safe. Where had that come from? Owen wondered. He felt tender toward Bailey, and excited to hold her. Was this a reaction to the fact that she was bearing his children? In a phenomenon known as couvade syndrome, dads-to-be experienced pregnancy symptoms such as morning sickness and mood swings. But he didn't think that was it.

She wriggled out of his arms. "Silly idea."

"What?" He tried in vain to recall the thread of their conversation.

"Playing nurse and doctor." She snatched her clothes from a chair. "Time for you to go do whatever world-famous doctors do on Friday nights."

"Eat dinner. Sing duets."

"Wouldn't that be a quartet, at this point?" she teased.

"You're right. I can hear their little voices chorusing, 'Take me out to Waffle Heaven.'" Having inhaled tantalizing scents drifting across the rear wall of their property for the past three weeks, Owen could resist no longer.

"Oh, waffles! You're on." Bailey made shooing motions. "I can't change with you here! Wait outside."

"Don't be long. I missed lunch." But as he wheeled the

sonogram machine out of the room, Owen acknowledged that what he hungered for most wasn't some confection of fried batter, fruit and whipped cream.

Still, that seemed a good place to start.

BAILEY WAS CONCERNED about ending up in Owen's bedroom, but she had to risk it. After all, that was the only route to the spa.

Maple syrup—bacon—all sorts of lovely stuff filled her stomach by the time they came home. Inevitably, one of them, or possibly both, seized on the notion of taking a relaxing dip.

She figured they'd be safe as long as she scurried right through on her way outside. And that might have worked, if she'd ever made it that far.

The problem was having to share a bathroom. With doors on either side, it was hard to remember to lock them both, so she walked in on Owen just as he was pulling his skimpy trunks into place over those narrow hips. The sight stopped her cold. She should have retreated. Really, she should have, but there she stood.

Planning to change after she washed up, she'd thrown a short robe over her underpants, loosely belted at the waist. The robe used to be relatively modest in the days before pregnancy swelled her breasts. Now the panels gapped wide above the belt. As she and Owen stood there eyeing each other, their breathing echoing off the walls of the small bathroom, she could feel the belt untying of its own will and the sides of the robe sliding apart.

The instant his hands cupped her breasts and his thumbs made little circles around the nipples, she was lost. By the age of twenty-eight, she ought to know that a man's distractingly gentle mouth and wonderfully clever tongue promised nothing beyond fleeting pleasure. Actually,

Bailey did know that. But as Owen pushed the robe into free fall and drew her against his rock hard body, she didn't care.

"We're going to regret this," she murmured as he lifted her onto the counter, knocking his and her paraphernalia into the sink.

"We'll regret it more if we stop."

Did he have to be so logical? And so right? "Okay," she said.

He explored her, lifting his head from time to time to observe her reactions. Bailey glimpsed their movements in the side mirror—he had a far better view, of course—but mostly she got lost in the sensations. He was so big, in more ways than one. Tantalizing her, taking his time. Kissing her again and again, expertly parting her and thrusting himself inside her.

She'd never experienced such utter radiant bliss. Right from the start, too. How much better could it get?

To her amazement, she found out. The man moved with grace, never hurrying, instinctively caressing the right places to arouse waves of delight, and then pulling out for a cool moment before starting again. Best of all was the expression of wonder on his face, as if he, too, was reaching a new level.

I could love this man. I might love him already. How utterly strange to be discovering this while pregnant with another man's children, Bailey thought. Yet as Owen merged with her for the third or maybe the fourth time, it felt as if they were making the babies all over again.

She noticed a change in Owen's expression: thrilled disbelief, and then a wild loss of control as he pushed into her harder. She transformed, fusing with him, and his mounting ecstasy and explosion of joy became hers, too.

They rocked there, holding each other, Bailey nearly

sliding off the counter and Owen making deep moaning noises that vibrated like music. For a long while, the world stood still.

At last he eased back. "What do you say we dispense with clothing for the spa?"

The walls around the yard were high, not to mention the thick shrubbery. "Sounds like a plan," Bailey said as he carefully lifted her down.

They soaked in the warm water, blissfully naked, then went inside and made love again in Owen's big bed. Afterward, curled against him with her bulge tucked against his hip, Bailey drifted in a happy haze.

Maybe it couldn't last. But it might for a while.

At 2:27 a.m. by the bedside clock, the rumble of delivery trucks woke Owen. He'd forgotten his earplugs.

The racket failed to stir Bailey, thanks no doubt to maternal hormones. She'd rolled over, facing away, her hair tangled across the pillow.

Owen lay on his back, trying to understand why he didn't have the awkward sense of displacement he usually got when he awoke beside a woman. Not that he ever picked up strangers. His affairs had been carefully chosen, with women he knew well enough to be certain there'd be no misplaced expectations.

Always, there was a constraint, like when he sat in front of the cameras and had to remember to keep his shoulders straight, his gaze forward and his language clear. In the morning, he would be careful with the lady. Carefully polite, cautious not to make assumptions, and ready to escape as soon as he could diplomatically do so.

He had no idea what to expect with Bailey. She might kick him out of bed in the morning, even though it was his bed, or she might race him to the shower. As for escaping, he wished he didn't have surgeries scheduled starting at 9:00 a.m. They'd brought home an extra waffle, and he wanted to enjoy it with her, slowly.

And with the babies. Yesterday…the ultrasound…his and her children. Those silly little people already loved the same music their parents did.

Their parents. What a powerful connection he'd forged with those babies. Boone hadn't seen them, hadn't shown any interest in the pregnancy as far as Owen could tell. The idiot acted as if he couldn't care less.

When the man returned from wherever he'd gone, Owen needed to have a straight talk with him. *Declare your intentions.* Old-fashioned, but appropriate.

If his brother wasn't prepared to love these children, then it would be time to tell Bailey the truth, and let the chips fall where they may.

BAILEY AWOKE TO THE SOUND of a phone ringing. Two phones, one close by and the other in the next room. She recognized the nearby ring tone as Owen's, while from afar came the pop tune she'd reserved for her sister's calls.

"Yes?" said Owen's deep voice, right beside her. "Cancelled? When's the second one? Right. I'll see you then. Thanks, Erica."

Bailey sat up. Her phone had gone silent. Why was Phyllis calling at…she checked the clock—7:29 a.m. on a Saturday?

"Good news," Owen reported. "My first patient got pregnant and won't need surgery. That doesn't explain why she failed to tell anybody until late last night, but we can fight over our waffle in peace. How about if I cut it, seeing as I'm such a fine surgeon, and you get first choice of halves?"

"It's too early in the morning for logic," Bailey grumbled. Who would have imagined that the tyrant of the operating room awoke in a cheery mood? Of course, some men were that way after they had sock-flinging sex. Make that robe-flinging sex. "I have to go find out what Phyllis wants."

"Be my guest."

She stumbled out of bed, poked around for her slippers before remembering she hadn't brought them in, and padded through the bathroom, which was the shortest route to her purse. At some point, they'd straightened the counter, but the image of the two of them going at it must be permanently etched into the mirror, likely to reappear outlined in steam the next time anyone took a shower.

Bailey dug out the phone. Pressing a button, she sat on a chair to wait. Honestly, that futon was way too low down. She might have to sleep in Owen's bed for the duration.

She waited for the call to connect. It did, then rang repeatedly.

Phyllis had called only minutes before. Why wasn't she answering?

Just as Bailey expected the call to go to voice mail, she heard her sister, but she seemed to be addressing someone else. "Thank you. This is important! I really appreciate... Bailey?"

"What's going on?"

"You have to help me!" Phyllis sounded in panic mode. "The police have this all wrong."

The police? "Have what all wrong?"

"They came busting in at some unearthly hour and dragged me out of bed. They won't tell me anything except I'm being booked for fraud." In the background, Bailey heard an ominous clang, like something out of a prison movie. "I heard somebody mention money being moved around, that that's why they had to take me in, and somebody else told him to put a lid on it. You have to bail me out! And get a lawyer."

Phyllis had been arrested. "Where are you?" Bailey asked.

"The Safe Harbor police department. They have this little jail here and I for sure don't want to be dragged down to the county lockup. I need help *now*."

Behind Bailey, Owen had come into the room, wearing a short silk robe. She struggled to figure out what to do. "How much is bail?"

"A hundred thousand dollars."

"What!" Bailey couldn't believe it. "I wouldn't know where to find that kind of money. Or even a tenth of it." She'd read an article once about bail bondsmen, and had the impression you paid them ten percent of the money they put up for bail. And while most bail got returned once the person showed up for court, that ten percent was gone forever.

"Just do it!" Phyllis was crying, and angry, too, but not at Bailey, she could tell.

Owen leaned in the doorway. "Tell me," he said.

Her first thought was to close ranks, that this was a family matter. But he was family. "I'll see what I can do," she told her sister. "Don't freak out."

"I'm counting on you!"

"I know. See you soon." Bailey clicked off.

Owen folded his arms. "Well?"

"She's been arrested." Bailey filled in as much as she'd learned. "What do I do?"

"*We* get a lawyer and have bail reduced." Owen took his own phone from his pocket. "I'll ask the hospital attorney for a recommendation."

"Oh! That's a good idea." She'd forgotten all about

Tony Franco. He handled the hospital's affairs but was also Nora's brother-in-law.

Owen paused with the cell in his hand. "What about Boone? Was he arrested, too?"

"I…I forgot to ask. But I don't think so. She didn't mention him." With a sinking feeling, Bailey remembered Owen saying that he didn't trust his brother. And judging by his scowl, these events didn't surprise him nearly as much as she would have expected.

Fraud, Phyllis had said. Which meant Bailey's savings might be gone, stolen by the people she'd trusted most.

Stolen by a man whose babies were wriggling inside her right this very minute.

Chapter Thirteen

Owen had never seen Bailey so distraught. Thank goodness he was here, he thought as he reached Tony at home, then put in a call to the recommended attorney, a fellow named Joseph Noriega. To the man's credit, he didn't hesitate to jump in to the case on a Saturday morning and promised to call back after checking into the situation.

"I need to go down and get Phyllis out," Bailey said for the umpteenth time. She'd been pacing through the house in anguish, barely taking time to shower, dress and down a bite of breakfast.

"You can't get her out until the lawyer arranges bail," Owen explained, also for the umpteenth time.

"A hundred thousand dollars! They have to reduce it." Her face had gone pale. "They can't consider her a flight risk, can they?"

"If Boone's left the country, they'll assume she might join him." Owen had learned that much during his brief conversation with the attorney.

Bailey plopped onto the living room couch, her reddish-brown hair curling wildly around her face. *Why did this have to happen on our first real morning together?* Owen grumbled inwardly. But he knew why, sort of.

Bailey's next words pricked his conscience. "I don't understand their rush. Whatever's happened, I'm sure Phyllis and Boone intend to make good on the investments if they possibly can."

Owen sat beside her. Time to reveal at least one of his secrets. "I'm afraid this is partly my...doing." He'd nearly said "fault," but the fault lay with Boone, not him.

"What do you mean?"

"Boone's father was a con man, and I thought I recognized the signs of someone preparing a swindle. Maybe I overreacted, but I felt a responsibility to those senior citizen investors." *And to you,* Owen nearly added, but he didn't want to lay any of the blame on Bailey. "I discussed my concerns with a fraud investigator at the police department."

"When?" Her eyes shone a luminous green in the morning light.

He couldn't read anything into her response. Not anger, not resentment, but not forgiveness, either. "About a week and a half ago."

She let out a long breath. "That's a relief."

"Why?" he asked in astonishment.

She peered at him guiltily. "Because a couple of weeks ago I said a few things to Nora and I'm sure she told Leo. I was afraid this was all *my* doing. But it was both of us."

Financial investigations didn't happen overnight, Owen suspected. "They've probably been looking into this for quite a while. Long before you or I—" His phone rang. "That might be the lawyer."

It was. Noriega had accomplished a remarkable amount in a few hours, as it turned out.

"I can't get bail reduced. There's too great a risk she'll skip the country."

"Why?" Owen asked.

"Apparently Mr. Storey's actions triggered the arrest— something to do with trying to move accounts the police have been monitoring," the lawyer explained.

Monitoring. That supported Owen's belief that this investigation hadn't just started in the past few weeks. "Move them where?"

"Offshore," the man said. "So his wife is definitely a risk to leave the country and join him overseas. However, as bail, the court will accept a lien against the couple's half ownership in that house you mentioned."

Great. Owen could end up co-owning this place with the state of California. However, since the attorney had explained that bail money had to be demonstrably clean— not illegally obtained—he saw no reasonable alternative. "If that's what Mrs. Storey wants to do, it's fine with me," he said.

"I'll confirm it with her and make the arrangements," Noriega said.

"I'm due in surgery, but Mrs. Storey's sister can meet you at the jail." Owen glanced at Bailey, who nodded.

As he filled her in on the latest news, he watched her turn even paler than before. "Boone's moving accounts offshore? He really is a con man. You were right."

"Let's not jump to conclusions." Hearing his own words, Owen shook his head. "But yes, I believe he is. It's better if we face facts."

"Not Phyllis!" Bailey flared. "She'd never cheat people."

From what he'd seen of his sister-in-law, Owen tended to agree. "Perhaps not. But she chose to believe what was in her own self-interest."

"She trusted the man she loved!" No question about where Bailey's loyalties lay.

"Granted." Owen didn't want to argue. "Bailey...you may have some hard decisions to make as a result of all this."

"Hard decisions?" Her forehead puckered obstinately. "I'm standing by my sister. What's hard about that?"

It was the wrong time to tell her about the babies' paternity. Besides, she hadn't entered this pregnancy with the intention of raising two children herself, any more than Owen had. "Nothing, for the moment. I'll be in touch with you later. Let me know if you need anything."

"Thanks. You've been great about all this." Bailey let him help her to her feet, a not-so-simple task. "This isn't exactly your problem, but I'm glad you're here."

"For a change?" he teased.

She slid her arms around his waist and Owen pulled her close, pressing his cheek into her hair. "For...however long you're around," he thought he heard her say, but the words were muffled.

"I'm not going anywhere," he told her. "Except to surgery."

"Right." Stepping back, she gave him a little salute. "Go help make some woman's dreams come true, Doc."

All the way to the hospital, he carried that image of Bailey standing in the living room, a small, brave figure prepared to do battle with whatever forces were arrayed against her family.

A family of which he was a part. Whether she truly accepted that or not.

FORTUNATELY, PHYLLIS'S NAME turned out to be on the house's title papers along with her husband's, and by midday the attorney got her released. Bailey was waiting with a hug and a ride back to the rented mansion by the harbor.

"I don't understand why I haven't heard from Boone." Phyllis had reverted to a childhood habit of chewing her lips. "I sent emails and texts, but you know how things are when you travel. Sometimes stuff doesn't get through."

Much as Bailey wished she could go along with her sister's excuses, she couldn't. "Email works fine overseas," she said. "When's the last time you heard from him?"

"A few days." In the passenger seat, Phyllis twisted a strand of blond hair.

"Where is he?" Bailey halted at a red light.

"He told me he was going to New Zealand, but Mr. Noriega says he's supposedly on some Caribbean island. Something about having a bank account there, but I didn't know anything about that. He'd have told me." Phyllis spoke fast, chattering in her nervousness.

"It's not one of those islands like in the movies where people keep secret bank accounts to launder stolen money, is it?" Bailey blurted.

Her sister shot her a sharp look. "That's Switzerland. And Boone wouldn't do such a thing. This is all a misunderstanding."

"Owen says…" Bailey broke off. It wasn't right to repeat hurtful gossip.

"Owen says what?" Phyllis demanded.

"Just…" She might as well finish what she'd started. "That Boone's father was a con artist. That he used to scam people."

"Owen's turning on his own brother?" Phyllis folded her arms furiously. "Exactly what I'd expect from Dr. Hoity-Toity. He thinks he's better than everyone else."

"He does not!" Okay, fair was fair. "Much."

"When exactly did he share this ugly nonsense about Boone's father with you, anyway?" Phyllis asked. "You two have gotten awfully chummy."

"*Someone* arranged for us to live together," Bailey pointed out.

"It was a misunderstanding."

"There seem to be a lot of misunderstandings going around." Bailey hadn't meant to be hard on her sister, especially under the circumstances, but she couldn't help it. "Phyllis, I invested my lifesavings with you guys."

"And you'll get them back, with a big profit, if the cops don't close us down prematurely!"

"Are you certain of that?"

The question hung in the air. Phyllis's mouth worked a few times before she said, "I can't believe it. My own sister is against me."

"I am not!" Bailey said.

"That didn't sound like loyalty to me!"

Bailey's gut tightened. They hadn't had much, growing up—a series of stepfathers and their mother's live-in boyfriends, one rundown apartment after another, an ever-changing panorama of schools, teachers and casual friends, at least until high school. As a result, she, Phyllis and their mother had formed a tight triangle. Loyalty had meant everything. And after their mother's death from a stroke five years ago, that had left the pair of them.

Until Boone came along. Of course, Bailey had accepted and supported her sister's marriage. But Owen was right. The guy didn't deserve their trust. Police weren't fools. They hadn't jumped into this investigation on a whim.

"Phyllis," she said, "no one has ever been more loyal to you than I am. I'm just not so sure about your husband."

That stubborn chin jutted out in a familiar gesture. "Owen's always been jealous of his big brother. Boone's dad was smart, and he knew how to make money. Owen's father could barely rub two coins together. Boone told me his dad used to buy him expensive presents, and Owen resented it. That's what this is about."

"I don't believe that." Bailey turned onto the drive that

ran along the harbor. It startled her how normal everything looked, a typical Saturday with sailboats and people fishing from the pier. "Owen's had plenty of reason to be upset."

"Such as?" Phyllis probed.

"Such as you two haven't paid my doctor bills and I didn't get my three-month checkup. Pregnancy is a serious business, especially when there are multiple babies involved." In the face of her sister's skeptical expression, Bailey added, "They mean a lot to Owen."

"Oh. *Now* I get it."

"Now you get what?"

"He told you," Phyllis said.

Told me what? Normally, Bailey would have blurted the question, but she'd begun forming a new habit: thinking before she spoke.

A couple of times, she'd caught odd glances between Phyllis and Owen. She'd dismissed the notion that they were up to something, figuring she'd misinterpreted, but now she realized that she had sensed some kind of secret. Something they hadn't told her.

If she let on that she was still in the dark, Phyllis would beat a hasty retreat. And Bailey would have a devil of a time finding out whatever these two were hiding.

What could it be? Some financial arrangement? That seemed unlikely. Then Bailey recalled that, right before her sister's puzzling statement, she'd been talking about the twins and how much they meant to their uncle. Could this have to do with the babies?

Whatever was going on, she didn't believe Owen had been manipulating her. He was straightforward to a fault, venting his moods openly. Sure, he needed to learn tact, but at least he wasn't sneaky like Boone, who smiled, shook your hand and paid you compliments while scheming to steal your money.

Well, if she hoped to get any information out of Phyllis, she'd have to play this carefully. "Yes, he told me," Bailey said, and cut off her impulse to follow that statement with a string of chatter. Nora had told her once about an investigative technique Leo used in interrogating suspects. It was called silence.

People hated silence. They wanted to fill it up. Bailey knew plenty about that, she reflected wryly, because in the past she'd been talkative to a fault. Thank goodness they were stuck in a line of traffic as sightseers and tourists hunted for parking spaces. Phyllis had nowhere to go and nothing else to do except talk.

A moment ticked by. "You're not mad?"

Bailey shrugged and kept her gaze on the car ahead of them.

"I don't blame you," Phyllis said. "But what was the difference, really? It's not like we cooked this up to take advantage of you. We discovered Boone's low sperm count early in the process of trying to have kids. Donating didn't seem to bother Owen. But then I ran into problems with miscarrying, as you know. So we already had the sperm whether I carried the baby or you did."

Owen was the father of her children? Bailey could hardly breathe.

During those ultrasounds, no wonder he'd stared raptly at the screen. And that explained his intense concern about her prenatal care, his interest in the babies' gender, even the way he'd pampered her at home. It wasn't her, Bailey, that inspired him. It was the fact that she was carrying his children.

All this while, he'd known. And hadn't said a word.

"Don't think this lets you off the hook for anything,"

Phyllis warned. "Boone's still their father for all practical purposes."

Bailey might be having trouble sorting out her feelings about Owen, but she had no hesitation regarding her brother-in-law. "Their father?" she snapped. "He's shown zero interest in these children and you know it. Not once did he go to the doctor with us. And considering that he's got money in an offshore account, he could have paid for my obstetrical care to ensure their safety. Now he's flown the coop, dumped you and me and the babies. Stop defending him, Phyllis. Even if it were his sperm, he's a lousy excuse for a father."

Her sister stared at her in shock. Just then, the traffic cleared, and Bailey was able to pull into the driveway of the fabulous, ridiculously overpriced rental mansion. To her, it seemed just another piece of evidence condemning her brother-in-law.

Phyllis didn't move. When Bailey looked again, she saw tears trembling in her sister's eyes.

"I'm sorry," Phyllis whispered. "I didn't know you felt that way."

"I didn't know I did, either."

A deep breath, and Phyllis straightened her shoulders. Defeat never lasted long in the Wayne household. "He's coming back, Bailey. He loves me, and he's honestly trying to save this project."

"What evidence do you have besides wishful thinking?" Bailey's own harshness surprised her. Being around Owen must have rubbed off on her.

"I've been married to him for three years," Phyllis said. "He told me he's never known anyone before that he felt truly at home with. We've faced setbacks, but we always vowed we'd tackle them together. And we have."

"Maybe he meant it, in his way," Bailey conceded. She'd

enjoyed Boone's company plenty of times, laughing at his quirky sense of humor, basking in the sense of belonging to this man's circle. He loved to entertain, and at the parties he and Phyllis had thrown, people flocked around him. Charismatic, that was the word for Boone Storey. How easy it was to get sucked in by him.

"You have to stick by me, you of all people." Phyllis wiped her eyes with the back of her hand. "Bailey, I love my husband and I love those babies, too. I'm forty years old. This is the only chance I'll ever have to become a mom. Don't take that away from me."

That contract...it had specified that Bailey was to be inseminated with Boone's sperm. The contract must be null and void, but even if a lawyer confirmed it, where did that leave her? With a sister whose heart was breaking and two babies in need of parents.

Even after she and Owen became lovers, he'd hidden the truth. While he might have some paternal feelings, he clearly had no intention of stepping up to be a father in the fullest sense of the word.

For a moment, Bailey entertained a fantasy. Her and Owen, married. Curling up in bed every night, fixing breakfast for their little boy and girl in the morning. Eating lunch together at the hospital cafeteria. Attending social events.

The great surgeon and his wife, the nurse. *The wife he had to marry because he got her pregnant.* That wasn't exactly how it went, but close enough. He hadn't chosen her. They'd been thrown together, sharing living quarters, sharing these babies. Even if Dr. T. did marry a woman so unlike the ladies he'd dated in Boston, everyone would know he hadn't actually chosen her.

Bailey took a deep breath and turned to face her sister in the front seat. "These are your babies," she said. "I conceived them for you and I'm carrying them for you. I just hope you don't have to go to prison."

"I won't!" Phyllis threw her arms around Bailey. "It will come out all right, you'll see. They're wrong about Boone. And you're making the right decision. Thank you, Bailey. I love you."

"I love you, too."

It was the right choice, Bailey told herself as they got out and went into the house. She was going to stand by her sister, and pray that everything somehow worked itself out.

If that made her guilty of wishful thinking like Phyllis, well, that might not be such an undesirable trait, after all.

Chapter Fourteen

Living in fast-forward mode suited Owen fine. He had the ability to focus on the moment even in the face of pressing responsibilities, particularly when performing surgery, then propel himself forward to the next task. Monday morning was no different. He completed two tricky operations by 10:00 a.m. and arrived at his office braced for more action.

Ned was ready for him, up to speed on the patients and prepared for the day's procedures. He must have consulted with Bailey, because he seemed confident without being cocky, as if certain he'd made the correct arrangements. And he had.

Owen tried hard not to dislike the guy. Ned aimed to please, and he had all the qualities a doctor required of a good nurse. It was the idea that he'd been able to talk to Bailey that chafed, because Owen had scarcely caught a glimpse of her since Saturday.

She'd basically moved in with her sister. Phyllis deserved the support, Bailey had explained Saturday night, when he returned home to find her stuffing odds and ends in a suitcase. "Someone has to look after her."

"That's fine, but who's going to take care of *you?*" he'd replied more sharply than he'd intended.

"She'll do that. She's committed to these babies." Her

tone implied something further, which was unusual for Bailey. Owen almost got the feeling she was making a dig at him, yet he'd never known Bailey to be anything but up-front with her feelings.

He hated to see her vanish into that mansion. He'd been looking forward to spending another night tangled in each other's arms. "You don't have to sleep there."

"It's a big place. She shouldn't be alone at a time like this."

"She's been alone all week and done fine," he'd grumbled.

"That was before she had a prison sentence hanging over her head and the whole world convinced her husband is a crook."

"The whole world?" The case hardly seemed that earth-shattering. As of Saturday afternoon, Owen hadn't heard a word about it on the radio or via the hospital grapevine.

"See you," Bailey had responded, and scampered out of the house so fast she left a breeze.

This morning, as Owen grabbed a bear claw pastry in the cafeteria, he'd seen her again, talking earnestly with Nora. He'd hesitated, trying to devise a suitable excuse for interrupting, and Dr. Sargent had joined the two of them. Since Owen hoped they were making arrangements for Bailey's maternity care, he'd decided to stay out of it.

But the situation was becoming intolerable, he decided between seeing patients that afternoon. Everybody including Bailey considered him an outsider—well, peripheral, anyway. Except that those were *his* children.

He had to find out what she intended to do with the twins. Surely she didn't still plan to hand them over to his con man of a brother.

He also had to level with her about his paternity, and

then they'd work something out. Owen hadn't come up with any brilliant ideas yet, but he expected to.

And he wanted Bailey to come home. He missed her cute little smile and smart-aleck approach to housekeeping. Also, he needed someone to put him in his place. For the first time in his life, Owen wished the staff wouldn't treat him with quite so much deference. It fed his giant ego, and that, he'd been learning, wasn't necessarily a good thing.

At five o'clock, he finally caught a break. Generally, he didn't eat until later, but he was hungry. Carrying his tray across the almost empty hospital cafeteria, Owen spotted her.

Elbows propped on a table, she sat staring into space across a plate of half-eaten pasta. He had her now. She'd never leave without finishing her meal; he knew her better than that.

His tray clunked as he dropped it onto the table. Smiling at her startled expression, Owen sat across from her. "Long time no see."

"We shouldn't be eating together in public," she protested.

No sense getting into a fruitless argument. "How's your sister?" he asked, popping open a milk carton.

"I don't know."

"Why not? You're living with her."

"She's been tied up all day."

"In court?" He had the impression criminal charges had to be presented promptly.

"They postponed her arraignment at her attorney's request. The D.A. wanted a meeting with her. That's all I know." Bailey glanced at the overhead clock. "I expected to hear from her by now."

"It wouldn't surprise me if they cut a deal," Owen said.

"Pit Phyllis against Boone?" Bailey blew out a disbelieving breath. "She'd never do that."

"Too foolishly trusting?" he asked.

"Too loyal!" Bailey returned.

Owen decided to cover one other, less touchy, matter before he broached what was uppermost in his mind. "Are you switching your medical provider? I saw you talking to Dr. Sargent."

Bailey poked at her pasta with her fork. "Yes. Nora suggested it, and he's agreeable. Under the circumstances, there's no point in my continuing to drive into L.A."

"Excellent."

He waited, expecting her to elaborate on the topic, but she didn't. Although she seemed to almost quiver with impatience, she remained silent.

Owen had no idea what she expected him to say. Bailey would no doubt let him know in her own sweet time, so he dug into his meat loaf and potatoes.

Seconds stretched into minutes. Finally she broke. "Weren't you ever going to tell me?"

"Tell you what?"

She shot him an irritated glance. To Owen's recollection, no one had looked at him with such exasperation since he was an intern. "Phyllis spilled the beans." She leaned forward. "About the sperm. You rat. You should have told me."

In a flash, Owen realized that he should have seen this coming, and should have taken care of it long ago. *But I meant to... It was on the tip of my tongue...* All true, but hardly credible. "I'm sorry."

"It's pretty obvious why you didn't," she went on with an uncharacteristic trace of bitterness.

"It's a touchy situation," he began.

"Oh, cut the crap." Bailey blinked, and to his dismay

he realized she was on the verge of tears. "In spite of everything we've…" She swallowed. "I know I'm not on your level intellectually or socially, or…."

What on earth was she talking about? "This has nothing to do with that," Owen said. "You're precious."

"It was the babies that fascinated you." If she mashed that pasta any harder, it would fuse with the plate. "And the fact that you're a big fat important father, in the scientific sense of the word. To you, I'm nothing but a…a convenient…surrogate!"

Tears slid down her cheeks. Owen ached to gather her close and reassure her, and the hospital grapevine be damned.

But matters weren't that simple. This was about as complicated a situation as he could imagine.

"I intend to stand by you," he said. "Whatever lies ahead, we'll deal with it together. This isn't something we can resolve emotionally, though. It's important to consider all the ramifications."

"How else can you resolve a situation like this except emotionally?" she retorted. "Oh, damn." That last was a reference to her phone playing a melody. "It's Phyllis."

Owen would gladly have strangled his sister-in-law for interrupting. Too late to object, though. Bailey had already taken the call.

"Hello? Well, of course it's me…. The what?" she said into the phone. "Sure, I do. Right now? Well, okay." Frowning, she clicked off.

"What's up?" Owen asked.

"She asked me to bring the first aid kit she gave me. You remember, it was in that gift basket."

Owen doubted Phyllis needed first aid. The toiletries he'd taken as a gesture of sisterly love and caring must have done double duty as a hiding place. "Bring it where?"

"Her lawyer's office, right now." Bailey stacked her dishes together.

What could a person hide in a first aid kit? "Did you open it? What's in there?"

"I have no idea." Bailey got to her feet. "You can bus my dishes for me. I'm in a hurry."

"Sure." Owen didn't mind being bossed around. It felt almost comfortable. "How about if we meet at home later and talk about this?"

"I don't know if I'll be back tonight."

"Bailey, you have to stop avoiding me."

"Not everything in the world is about you, Owen," she answered tightly, and off she went at a rolling pace.

As he watched her go, Owen caught a couple of very interested glances from fellow staffers. He responded with his coldest scowl, one that a former colleague had referred to as his They-might-find-your-body-at-the-bottom-of-the-harbor-if-you're-not-careful look.

He hoped it worked.

I INTEND TO STAND BY YOU. Easy words, Bailey thought grimly as she let herself into the house. Although she'd only been away for two days, it felt hollow and lonely, like a location from the distant past. A place where she used to be happy, until she discovered she'd been living in a fool's paradise.

What did Owen have against emotions, anyway? If he was worth his salt in the romantic sense, he should have thrown himself at her. That wasn't a silly fantasy—some men actually did that. Alec and Patty, for instance. He'd broken her heart in high school, but twelve years later he'd flung himself at her feet and begged her to take him back. Well, maybe it hadn't happened precisely that way, but that's how Bailey had imagined it when Patty showed her the engagement ring and glowed about how they'd finally come home to each other.

She could never truly come home to Owen. He wasn't capable of that kind of selfless love. No matter how he might convince himself that he was standing by her, it would only be in a practical and basically heartless way. By offering money, maybe. With plenty of strings attached when it came to the kids.

Under the bathroom sink, she found the kit, a small square box with a blue base and a white top embossed with a red *X*. Setting it on the counter, Bailey fought a brief battle with her curiosity.

Phyllis hadn't said anything about not opening it. Furthermore, it had been a gift, so technically it belonged to Bailey. On the other hand, she got the impression that her sister's future might depend on whatever lay inside.

"You're going to lose this fight, so get on with it," she muttered, and opened the box.

How disappointingly ordinary. Antiseptic cleansing wipes, plastic bandages in various sizes, chewable aspirin tablets, a cold compress, gauze, first aid tape, an American Red Cross first aid pamphlet, vinyl gloves, scissors, tweezers, a thermometer...

And, underneath, a computer memory stick.

Bailey regarded the small device with a sense of disbelief. Not because it was unusual; she owned several of the things herself for backing up her computer and sharing files with friends. But because, obviously, her sister had put it there intentionally.

She used me.

Okay, that wasn't the worst thing Phyllis had ever done. And Bailey supposed that, if you wanted to hide information, you wouldn't go telling your kid sister about it. It wasn't even that big a deal; Phyllis could just as easily have stored it online somewhere.

Except that if it was findable via her computer, then Boone might have located it. A physical memory stick, off the premises, lay beyond his access.

Had Phyllis been hiding information from the authorities, from Boone, or both? In any case, she'd chosen a place no one else was likely to look. All weekend, her sister had protested loud and long that she trusted and believed in her husband. That she'd stand by him and prove everyone wrong. Yet all the time, this little item had lurked beneath Bailey's bathroom sink, evidence that Phyllis had suspected something all along.

Well, people were waiting. Curious though she might be, Bailey didn't intend to compound her snooping by trying to read the thing. With her marginal computer skills, she might accidentally damage it or lose data, and then all hell would break loose. She might even become accessory to a crime.

She replaced everything in the kit the way she'd found it, or as near as possible. Taking the whole box, Bailey was about to rush to her car when she felt a prick of dread. Did carrying this apparent evidence of a crime put her in danger? Suppose Boone showed up and demanded she hand it over?

Maybe she was being paranoid, but Bailey peered through the window to make sure the coast was clear. Couldn't tell much through the overgrowth. After a moment's internal debate, she went in the kitchen and armed herself with a knife. Then she let herself out cautiously, alert to any sudden movement or unexpected sound.

Next door, a lawn mower started up. Bailey nearly jumped out of her flip-flops. Good thing the guy who lived there couldn't see her through the trees, or at least, she hoped not.

Walking fast, she made it to her car and locked herself inside. Then, with the knife beside her on the seat, she took off for the lawyer's office.

OWEN DIDN'T FIND OUT from Bailey what was in the first aid kit. And, when he arrived home Monday night, he saw no sign of her. Gone again. Loyal to her sister.

That didn't bode well, any way you looked at it. Sticking by Phyllis presumably meant sticking by Boone, as well. And even though he knew his brother was entitled to his day in court, the man's continued absence screamed "Guilty" louder than any jury foreman.

Unless something bad had befallen Boone. But Owen doubted that. His brother was top dog in any fight.

He hoped Phyllis had hidden some damn good evidence in that first aid kit. Much as he disliked the way she'd put her sister in the middle, at least she'd had the sense to protect herself.

On Tuesday, Ned's continuing cheerfulness grated on Owen once again. But the young man didn't seem to be hiding anything or smirking behind Owen's back, either. A carefully worded question, "Seen Bailey recently?" brought the artless response, "She's sticking like glue to that sister of hers. But you'd know more about that than I would."

That afternoon, Dr. Rayburn's secretary called and asked him to stop by the administrator's office as soon as he was free. Around two-thirty, Owen found himself sitting at a private conference table with Mark Rayburn and Jennifer Martin.

"Flash News/Global broke the word today that your brother's been arrested in the Caribbean on financial fraud charges," Mark said. Flash News was an internet wire service and video feed for which Jennifer's journalist husband had once worked.

"First I've heard of it." That had been quick, considering Boone's presumed elusiveness. Whatever information Phyllis had provided to the authorities, it must have been potent. "Is the news mentioning me by name?"

"So far, no," Jennifer said. Dark-haired, with a low, husky voice, the PR director could have been an appealing on-camera presence herself. "We ought to be prepared, just in case."

"Sorry to ask you this, but were you even tangentially involved in your brother's financial dealings?" The administrator's calm manner took the sting out of his words.

"Financial? No." The personal dealings were nobody's business. "I co-own a house with him and his wife, but that predates this whole business."

"Excellent." Mark leaned back. "I think we're in the clear."

Jennifer wasn't so easily reassured. "We may be all right if this blows over quickly, but if it gets bigger and lasts longer, it could affect the opening."

"Are you suggesting we delay?" Owen didn't like the idea. For one thing, he'd done nothing wrong. For another, a ton of work and planning had gone into the events scheduled to begin within a few weeks. "That feels like an overreaction to me."

"Agreed. A few weeks or a month isn't going to make any difference, anyway," Mark said, and Jennifer nodded slowly.

"Good," Owen said emphatically. "I'm sorry my half brother's got himself into this mess and hurt people, but we're doing important work here."

"That's a good line to take," Mark replied. "Keep the focus on the fact that you're helping people."

Jennifer shook her head. "Be careful. You don't want to be perceived as attacking your brother when he hasn't been convicted of anything yet."

That struck Owen as reasonable. "So I express concern about my brother and his activities, and hope that justice is done one way or the other. Is that bland and inoffensive enough?"

The others chuckled, Jennifer with a hint of nervousness. "It'll do," Mark said.

That hadn't gone badly, Owen reflected as he walked down the hall to his administrative office. No one had even mentioned Bailey. He wondered if they planned to brief her also, but he doubted that. It was unlikely the press would pay any attention to an obscure nurse.

Obscure. Didn't that mean vague, murky and ambiguous? Hardly the right words to describe someone so vital and forthright.

They needed to talk about the twins and their future. About what kind of home the babies should grow up in. About how to support them and cherish them. Owen smiled, remembering those little figures cavorting inside their mother on the sonogram. He missed sitting next to Bailey at the keyboard or on the couch, watching TV. He missed the awareness of his children being so close.

Get to work, Doc. You've got an opening to prepare for. He also had a paper to present at the conference scheduled the following month. As he'd said, this was important work.

Owen didn't come up for air until around 6:00 p.m. when his cell rang. It was Jennifer. "There's a camera crew outside the hospital asking to speak to you." She sounded uneasy. "You might want to slip out the back way."

"You're telling me to cut and run?" Owen couldn't believe she'd advise such a tactic.

"They have questions about your brother," Jennifer explained. "Somehow they made the connection to you. Remember Hayden O'Donnell, that fellow who interviewed you about the multiple birth?"

"Vaguely." The reporter had been rather pompous, but Owen supposed some people would describe him that way, too.

"Well, this is now an international news story and he believes anything that focuses on Safe Harbor is his territory. He's going to dig for as much dirt as he can."

Maybe Jennifer was right, but... "If they catch me sneaking out the doctors' entrance, it'll look even worse."

"We could take you away in an ambulance," Jennifer proposed.

That sounded like a scene from a TV comedy. "How about a helicopter?" he joked. The hospital did have a helipad on the roof.

"Okay, I was kidding. Sort of."

"Let them ask their questions. They'll get bored and move on." That had been Owen's experience with the press in a few previous cases where the public got worked up. One had concerned a doctor on his staff who'd eloped with a seventeen-year-old girl, and another had involved a mentally unstable woman who'd sued after he'd refused to provide fertility treatments. She'd later dropped the suit.

Still, he took a moment to compose himself and review what he knew about Boone's situation, which wasn't much. Then he splashed some water on his face, ran a comb through his hair and descended to the lobby.

"We'll be fine," he told Jennifer and Mark, who were waiting for him. The administrator was his usual unflustered self and, stepping out to find only one camera crew and a couple of reporters from local papers, Owen felt equally comfortable.

He didn't care for the way Hayden stuck a microphone in his face and intoned his questions as if the fate of the earth hung in the balance, but Owen easily dispatched the topic of his half brother—eight years older, different fathers—and the investment scam. "Until a few weeks ago, I hadn't seen my brother for several years," he said honestly. "We have zero financial dealings together aside from co-owning a house."

The reporter's face lit up as if he'd just been handed a Christmas present. "A house where you currently cohabit with the sister of your brother's wife, isn't that right?"

Where had the man dug up that bit of gossip? "We're sharing a house. It was unplanned. Her sister and my brother didn't communicate with each other when they each separately offered us a place to stay."

"I understand she's a nurse here and that she's pregnant— a surrogate for Boone and Phyllis Storey," O'Donnell said. "Did you perform the insemination, Dr. Tartikoff?"

Uh-oh. The guy was verging on dangerous territory. "A relative? Absolutely not. I never even met Miss Wayne until I arrived in Safe Harbor last month."

"Are you her physician?" O'Donnell probed.

"I am not."

"But you live together?"

"As I explained, we barely know each other."

"What a coincidence," the man said sarcastically. "The two of you set up cozy housekeeping here in Safe Harbor, while your brother and her sister are busy stealing forty million dollars."

Beside him, Owen heard a gasp from Jennifer. In that moment, a couple of points struck him.

First, he wondered how on earth Boone had managed to

steal that much money. Second, he realized that this was a bigger scandal than he'd imagined, and it wasn't going to go away anytime soon.

Third, he could see in O'Donnell's eyes that the man had more inflammatory questions, a whole sheaf of them, and that he was going to keep poking and probing as hard as he could.

Sneaking out the back way, ambulance or no, was beginning to sound like an option he should have considered a lot more seriously.

Chapter Fifteen

"Look at him." With the lid of her nail polish bottle, Phyllis gestured at the giant TV screen. "That suit's new, and it cost a bundle. Apparently he had an entire house full of stuff that I didn't know about. Possibly a whole private island. The only thing missing is some bimbo on his arm, but I'll bet he has a few of those stashed around, too."

"Yes, but look at his black eye," Bailey said. On the set, a handsome but bruised Boone, wrists manacled behind his back, was half led, half shoved through a crowd by a couple of tough-looking men. The caption bore the name of a Caribbean island called Isla del Diablo and Accused Scammer Waives Extradition.

"Apparently the one thing he failed to check out is how the thuggish dictator on Devil's Island treats fugitives. Especially fugitives who neglect to pay him off in advance," Phyllis muttered.

The newswoman's voice caught Bailey's attention. "After what appears to have been a rough night in a local jail, fugitive Boone Storey agreed to surrender to U.S. authorities to face charges in the theft of an estimated forty million dollars. The money was allegedly swindled from senior citizens in a spreading investment inquiry."

The newscast cut to a studio in Los Angeles, where a

blonde anchorwoman turned to a man beside her. "Forty million dollars. How much is that exactly, Burt?"

"A whole lot of coconuts," he said, and flashed white teeth as if he'd said something funny.

Bailey uttered a low growl. Grateful as she was that her brother-in-law had to face charges, she hated seeing her family business splashed out there for the whole world to mock.

Beside her, feet plopped on the teak coffee table, Phyllis resumed applying pink polish to her toenails. She hadn't even bothered to lay down a cloth to protect the furniture, Bailey noted unhappily. Just because the place was rented didn't make it okay to ruin things.

This entire entertainment room reeked of excess. The biggest, the newest, the fanciest equipment. A wet bar, a snack fridge, a popcorn stand—anything you could name. Soon, she had no doubt, Phyllis would be giving it up, but clearly her sister intended to enjoy it to the last possible moment.

"I can't believe you suspected what was going on and didn't try to stop him." Bailey had been aching to say that all evening.

Phyllis paused with the brush in the air. "Don't you start judging me."

"I'm not, but what do you consider me, your mule?"

"Mule?" Her sister cocked an eyebrow.

"That's what drug traffickers call the suckers who carry their junk for them and run all the risks," she said. "You used me to hide your evidence."

"Oh, that." Phyllis dabbed a spot she'd missed. "I'm not stupid. I could tell he was keeping secrets, and while I figured that's just his nature, I decided to back up all the information on his laptop. Usually he kept it password protected but one day he forgot to log off."

"Which doesn't explain why you hid the memory stick in my first aid kit," Bailey shot back.

"What better place to put it?" was her sister's unfazed response.

Bailey had had a rough twenty-four hours since presenting that evidence at the lawyer's office. He and Phyllis hadn't been the only ones present. A couple of people she gathered were prosecutors or high-level investigators had also sat around studying her as if she were an unindicted coconspirator. She'd practically flung the thing at Phyllis and fled.

Today at work, she'd heard murmurs when her back was turned, conversations in the hallways and cafeteria that stopped when she approached and resumed a moment later. Everybody seemed to know that she was pregnant with the children of this awful man. They acted as if it were somehow her fault he'd robbed all those people, when she'd been cheated of her lifesavings, too.

"There's no point frowning at me." Phyllis recapped the bottle. "I don't have the money. Boone spirited it away. It really frosts me that he ripped you off and double-crossed me."

"What about those old people?"

"The prosecutor says that with the data I turned over, they might be able to recover some of their money."

"Pennies on the dollar," Bailey muttered.

"Most likely." Phyllis brightened. "The good news is, for turning state's evidence, I might get a suspended sentence. I loved that crook, but I'm not going to prison for him."

"I hope not." Before Bailey could say more, a new image on the screen caught her attention. "Wait a minute!"

"Guess they connected the dots to Dr. High-and-Mighty." Phyllis upped the volume a few notches.

On the hospital steps, Owen stood, expression hovering

between impatience and indulgence. Trying to humor the press, Bailey gathered. A caption read "Dr. Owen Tartikoff, Brother of Former Fugitive Boone Storey."

"You cohabit with the sister of your brother's wife, isn't that right?" demanded a smug middle-aged reporter in what appeared to Bailey to be a heavily edited cut.

"We barely know each other," Owen answered snappishly.

"Did you own a share of his financial business?" A close-up of the reporter, identified as Hayden O'Donnell, might have been shot later and edited in, Bailey thought. Jennifer's husband, Ian, had once conducted a workshop for staff about how the press could alter your statements and take them out of context.

"Absolutely not. I arrived in Southern California a few weeks ago as director of Safe Harbor Medical Center's fertility program. My half brother and I were virtually estranged."

"Estranged?" Phyllis let out a hoot. "That liar!"

"He said 'virtually,'" Bailey felt obliged to note.

"What about the part where he barely knows you?"

She had a fierce sensory image of Owen making love to her on the bathroom counter, the two of them wrapped in each other, lost in the moment. Of course he couldn't mention that on television, but still...

"Let's get back to you sharing a house with Mrs. Storey's sister—the one who's pregnant with your brother's child," O'Donnell went on. "Is she really a surrogate or is your brother running some kind of harem?"

Phyllis let out a shriek, followed by a string of curse words. "How dare he!"

Bailey started to shiver. Could someone really say things like that about you on TV and get away with it?

"Of course she's a surrogate," Owen replied tautly. Why wasn't he outraged? Why didn't he call the man a jerk?

"But you had nothing to do with that?"

"With inseminating her? As I explained, I wouldn't do that with a family member."

"Now she's a family member," O'Donnell prodded. "I thought you hardly knew her."

"Miss Wayne is an excellent nurse at Safe Harbor," Owen answered coolly. "She is related to me by marriage, and coincidentally we found ourselves as housemates. There is nothing more to be said."

Finally, the camera cut back to the studio. Phyllis clicked off the set, which was a relief. Bailey didn't think she could bear to listen to any smirking chitchat between the anchorpersons.

"I didn't mean to put you in this position," Phyllis said.

"I know." Bailey sank deeper into the sofa. "You just wanted a baby."

Her sister placed a hand on her wrist. "I still do."

Miserably, Bailey voiced the doubts that had been assailing her. "They need a stable home. How can you take care of them both? You're broke, Phyllis. It'll be like us and Mom, maybe worse. At best, you'll be on probation, and people will sue you and you'll be notorious. It'll be years before you can have a normal life. And taking care of twins is hard on even settled families."

"Yeah, I've been thinking about that." Her sister wiggled her toes, as if to dry the polish faster. "You seem kind of attached, too. So why don't you give me the girl, and you can keep the boy? That way we each get one."

Bailey felt as if she'd dropped into a bad melodrama. "It doesn't work that way."

"What doesn't?"

"Children aren't puppies." Inside, her little guests chose

this inopportune moment to start squirming. "And I'm not a broodmare. Look how big I am already! What do you suppose my life's going to be like between now and January? I was counting on you to support me, financially and emotionally. If you can't do that, and I don't see how, then I'm going to have to make other plans."

"Other plans?" Phyllis went very hard. "You mean keep them both for yourself."

"Or find another home for them," Bailey flared. "One where the parents are ready to commit whatever it takes to raising their children."

"You and Owen cooked this up."

"Are you kidding? He barely knows me."

The weak attempt at humor flew right past Phyllis. "We made a deal. I get my pick of the kids."

Apparently her sister hadn't heard a word she'd said, Bailey thought in anguish. "We made a deal for me to bear children for you and Boone, and for the two of you to take responsibility for my prenatal care and for the child or children afterward. You've broken that deal so many ways I can't even count them."

Phyllis got to her feet. "Get out."

"What?"

"Out." Her sister glared. "You're just in this for what you can get. What is it, Bailey? You think I've got some secret stash of money I'm going to hand over to you? Or maybe you can find some rich couple who'll shower you with gifts so they can adopt *my* children? Well, I've heard enough. Get out of my house."

How could she think this? Bailey longed to point out how much she loved her sister and that they were family. *You can have the babies. Just don't shut me out.*

Except she couldn't. Because the twins were poking her with their little knees and elbows, reminding her of how helpless and needy they were. Tonight, their so-called father was in prison for being a worthless con man, their real father had practically disowned their mother, and Phyllis was treating them like a litter of prize pooches, up for sale to the highest bidder.

The only person who really cared was Bailey. She had to stand by them.

"I'm sorry you feel that way." With as much dignity as she could manage, she scooted forward on the couch and stood up. "I'll collect my things." She'd been staying in the bedroom next to Phyllis's because being alone in this big house scared her sister. Well, Bailey missed her own bed, even if it was a futon. Oh, heavens. How was she going to go back to sleeping on *that?*

"Let me know when you change your mind," Phyllis said.

"Let me know when you're going to act like a real mother," Bailey answered, and went to pack.

For the first time in her twenty-eight years, she felt older than her big sister. About a century older.

MUCH AS OWEN LONGED TO put the whole miserable press confrontation out of his mind, Mark Rayburn and Jennifer Martin had other ideas. "It's important to watch how they edit and treat this on the air," the public relations director told him.

So they, and from a distance Chandra Yashimoto, suffered through the nine and ten o'clock broadcasts. In the administrator's spacious office, Owen had to watch impassively as his older brother was manacled and taken into federal custody. Naturally, he joined the others in expressing dismay over Boone's crimes. Yet a part of him still loved the older brother who'd protected him when he was a kid, the brother he'd always hoped would escape the criminal patterns established by his father.

When Hayden O'Donnell's segment came on, Owen bristled at the man's insinuations about Bailey. So did Mark. "A harem? That man's gone over the edge."

Jennifer blew out a long breath. "It's embarrassing, but mostly for Boone. There's nothing here that puts you in a bad light, Owen."

"Just be careful," the vice-president added by teleconference. "Are you still sharing a house with this woman?"

Owen gritted his teeth at the term *this woman,* but held on to his temper. "Technically, yes, although she's been staying with her sister."

"Keep her at arm's length." Chandra's dark hair swung as she nodded emphatically. "Don't be seen with her in public. Dr. Rayburn, is it true she works at the hospital?"

"She works in Dr. Nora Franco's medical office," he clarified.

Owen felt himself go very still. If Chandra tried to get Bailey fired…

"And she's an outstanding, hardworking nurse," Mark went on. "As you'll recall, we have a policy in this hospital of supporting our people even when they make mistakes, as long as there's no intentional wrongdoing."

"Certainly." Chandra didn't appear mollified, though. "Still, if this woman continues to be a source of embarrassment, it might be time for her to consider going on early maternity leave. Fully paid, of course."

Owen had to clamp his jaw shut to keep from arguing. He had no right to speak for Bailey.

Fortunately, Mark wasn't finished. "Whenever Miss Wayne is physically and emotionally ready to start her maternity leave, I'll be happy to arrange it. And not a day sooner."

Chandra pressed her lips together. After a moment, she said, "Well, it's three hours later here, and I'm bushed. I'll trust you to handle things out there, Mark. You're the best judge of the situation."

Once she ended the call, Mark declared himself ready to turn in as well. "We may have to keep dodging bullets, but I hope the focus of attention will remain on your brother, Owen. I'm sorry about him, for your sake."

"Me, too," Jennifer added.

"Thanks." Although he rarely ran out of steam even by 11:00 p.m., tonight Owen felt unaccountably weary. It had been an emotional day. "See you both tomorrow."

He was getting into his car in the garage when it struck him why he'd had a nagging sense of déjà vu about that scene in Mark's office. Last December, Dr. Samantha Forrest had let slip to the press prematurely about Owen's being hired for this position. Since he hadn't yet revealed that information to his employers in Boston, it had been extremely awkward, and he'd insisted he would turn down the job unless Mark fired her. Despite pressure from above, Mark had stood up for his employee, a quality that Owen admired so much he'd decided to take the job anyway.

Now Dr. Sam—whose sometimes touchy friendship with Mark had blossomed and resulted in a very happy marriage——was one of his favorite people here at Safe Harbor. The fact that, as a pediatrician, she didn't have to work directly with Owen probably helped their friendship, he admitted with an inward smile as he drove through the quiet streets.

How easy it had seemed last December, with his lofty sense of remoteness, to imagine that one could easily control the press. Tonight, Owen had come within a knife's edge of lambasting O'Donnell on camera. Once your emotions got involved, everything changed.

He'd had half a mind to punch the guy out for that crack about the harem. It irked him that legally he'd be the one guilty of assault—not to mention the risk to his surgeon's hands—whereas in the old days a gentleman was expected to stand up for a lady's honor.

The closer Owen drew to the house on the cul de sac, the more he missed Bailey. And the more indignant he became on her behalf. Pregnant because she loved her sister, robbed of the savings that should have upgraded her career to nurse practitioner, and now belittled in the media—how utterly unfair. Why couldn't everyone see what a shiningly honest soul she was?

The sight of her unassuming compact in the driveway lifted his spirits. To be on the safe side, he glanced around for any sign of the press. No news vans cluttered the curb, and he doubted anyone would bother lurking in the bushes simply to watch him walk into a house where he'd already admitted he lived.

No one approached, and he let himself inside without incident. Everything lay quiet. Bailey's door was firmly shut, with no light showing beneath.

He knew he ought to mind his own business, but he couldn't resist opening it to peer in. A small figure lay curled on the futon, lightly covered. Nights tended to be cool this close to the ocean, but pregnant women generated heat. Speaking of her condition, someone ought to buy her a decent bed, or else a crane to help her in and out of this one as she grew bigger.

She didn't stir.

They had a lot to discuss. Owen wondered if she'd seen him on TV, and what she thought about that.

As he slid the door shut, he told himself they'd talk in the morning. He was looking forward to it.

Chapter Sixteen

The odd sound of a baritone voice singing, "I am sixteen going on seventeen..." in the shower woke Bailey, or perhaps she'd been rising into consciousness and that was simply the final straw. Why was a grown man singing a song written for a teenage girl?

She'd forgotten to wear earplugs. But she doubted that would have helped with him right in the next room.

As August sunlight slanted through the vertical blinds, she registered that she was back in the house on Morningstar Circle. Owen was here too, and in a fine mood.

In the shower, the melody shifted to "Oh, What a Beautiful Mornin'." Someone ought to slap that man. No one had a right to be so cheerful at seven o'clock in the morning.

Yet Bailey lay there relishing the deep reverberation of his voice and the sense of his nearness. It occurred to her that making love in the bathroom might have been a mistake, in the sense that she had a hard time putting those vivid scenes out of her mind when she ought to be thinking about ordinary stuff like brushing her teeth or whether she could sneak in there and use the facilities while he was otherwise occupied. She kept thinking about inviting herself into the warm water and his arms...

Except that she couldn't afford to be blithe, impulsive

Bailey any more. Her easygoing nature had landed her in a huge mess and, like it or not, Owen was part of it.

Unhappily, Bailey lay there until the water stopped. She followed the sounds as he dried off and moved away, humming. Finally, she heard his closet door open, which meant the bathroom was free.

With speed born of desperation, Bailey lumbered out of bed, opened the door on her side, stumped across the small bathroom and locked the access to his bedroom. She did the same to hers, for good measure.

"Hey!" came a laughing protest. "Share!"

"You had your turn!"

"I need my blow-dryer. My hair's going to dry all messed up."

"Run your fingers through it like any normal guy. Buy an extra brush." Why was she giving suggestions to a grown man? "Suck it up."

He laughed.

When Bailey emerged half an hour later, she followed the scent of cinnamon into the kitchen. Two gooey bear claws dripping with sugar and other enticing, health-free enhancements were warming in the toaster oven, while Owen sat drinking coffee and reading the morning paper.

If only the front page hadn't been staring her in the face, Bailey might have enjoyed a few more minutes before reality intruded. Instead, she had to stomach the sight of Boone's defiant expression beneath a Fugitive Captured headline.

Owen lowered the paper. He looked nothing like his brother, she reflected. His eyes brimmed with welcome and he gave her an off-center grin. "Welcome home, princess."

"Better be careful. Someone might see you talking to me." Bailey hadn't meant to snap at him. "Tell me one of those pastries is mine and I promise not to bite you at least until I finish eating it."

"It is. I bought them at the cafeteria last night. Two-for-one because they were past their prime, but the toaster perks them right up." He transferred them onto plates he'd set out.

"Thanks." Bailey sat down.

"Don't take this the wrong way, but why are you back?"

"Phyllis is being a jerk."

"I assumed something of the kind," he said, and waited.

Bailey relished a long, delicious mouthful before admitting, "She actually proposed that I split up the babies. Give her the girl and keep the boy. As if they were a litter of puppies!"

"Be honest," Owen said. "If she'd offered to let you keep the girl—"

"Absolutely not!" she flared.

"That was a joke."

"Not funny." Glumly, she peered out the window into the side yard. Old gardening tools, a decrepit ladder, a hideous lawn gnome...left by former renters, she presumed. A gorgeous fuchsia hung in a pot, hooked up to the automatic watering system.

"Did you catch me on the news last night?" he asked.

Surely the man didn't expect praise! "I learned quite a few things," Bailey said.

"Oh?" He fixed his full attention on her.

"Such as that we hardly know each other." To her dismay, she felt the sting of tears. What was wrong with her?

"That's true as far as it goes. We only met a few weeks ago. And that was more or less by accident."

"In other words, you didn't choose me." Bailey took a couple of quick breaths to regain control.

"Choose you for what?"

To be your lover. I was convenient, that's all. But he'd never said otherwise, had he? Hadn't made promises or claimed to be in love with her. Hadn't even bothered to tell her that these babies were his. "Anything."

"Why won't you look at me?" he asked.

She was staring out the window, trying not to cry. And getting mad. Why was he torturing her? "I answered your question. Yes, I caught you on the news."

"You don't sound like yourself," Owen said.

Time to quit dodging his gaze. Stiffening her resolve, Bailey faced him. "That's right. I've changed. I've become a person who has two children that depend on me and nobody else."

He laid his hand gently over hers. "You don't have to handle this alone."

In her heart, hope stirred, painfully, like blood circulating through a limb that had fallen asleep. "What do you mean?"

"I can help you figure out a plan," Owen said.

"A plan?"

"Financial arrangements. So you can keep the twins." He spoke with satisfaction, as if he'd worked everything out.

"I don't want your money, if that's what you're offering," Bailey snapped, and got to her feet. "These are your kids, but that doesn't seem to matter to you."

She couldn't bear to be around this man for one more minute. He didn't love her, and he never would. She wasn't his type, just some woman who'd gotten pregnant with his children through none of his doing. A woman he'd taken to bed since she happened to live in the next room. As far as she could tell, the man didn't have a heart at all, whereas hers was aching and throbbing as if it might burst right out of her body any second.

"Don't be unreasonable," Owen said. "We have to keep things quiet, at least for now."

"Don't worry!" she snapped. "I'm not going to embarrass you. I'm sure we've all been publicly humiliated enough to last a lifetime."

Then she stomped away.

"KEEP HER AT ARM'S LENGTH."

Yes, he'd done a great job of that, hadn't he? Owen reflected grimly as he drove to work. Much as he hated seeing Bailey in pain, he hadn't gone after her. Not that it would have done any good, under the circumstances. Besides, he had surgery scheduled.

He had no idea what he could have said. How to explain, to her or himself, this powerful urge to shelter her and the babies, even though the timing was terrible and he had an overriding responsibility to the hospital's program.

If Owen publicly revealed his paternity, the scandal would explode far beyond anything he'd imagined previously. With Boone's arrest making headlines nationally, the press would have a field day. The fallout wouldn't just tarnish his reputation or hurt Bailey, it would harm a lot of other people, too.

That day, Owen found himself regarding his colleagues in a new light. Erica Benford had moved from Boston to work with him. Alec Denny had relocated his daughter and was planning to marry and settle down, secure in his position as director of laboratories. Jan Garcia had likely given notice at her cryobank in Houston after accepting his job offer. Even Ned Norwalk was turning himself inside out to learn Owen's preferences and keep his medical office running smoothly.

All these people depended on him, as did the patients who put themselves in his hands. They trusted him and the team he was pulling together to bring their dreams to fruition.

Difficult as it was, he had to hold back. Bailey had friends who'd loved her and cared about her long before Owen came on the scene. In a few months, after the press turned its attention elsewhere, there'd be plenty of time for him to step back into the picture and help her figure out how to proceed with the twins.

That night, when he arrived home late and found her possessions gone, the house shivered with her absence. Owen nearly changed his mind. If he called enough people, surely he could find her.

But his brain told him that was the wrong step to take.

"WHY DIDN'T YOU HAVE any more children? Or is that too personal a question?" Bailey curled up on Renée Green's dainty couch, trying not to disturb the hand-crocheted doily on the arm.

The room belonged in a fairy-tale cottage. One wall was lined with china cabinets displaying shepherdesses, biblical figurines and small animals, while plates depicting Alpine villages and pastoral scenes filled another. Stenciled curlicues embellished the top of each doorway, and vases and bowls decorated with flower designs topped the end tables. Even her petite footstool bore a colorful painted bouquet.

"I don't mind you asking." The older woman leaned back in her armchair. "But it's hard to know where to begin."

While Bailey waited for Renée to organize her thoughts, she gave silent thanks for her new friend. After this morning's scene with Owen, she'd recognized an urgent need to find new quarters. She had lots of reasons, from the danger of being ambushed by the press to the fact that she no longer wanted to be dependent on Phyllis in any way. More than anything, she couldn't bear to keep waking up with only a thin wall separating her from the man she'd so unwisely fallen in love with.

At work, as she considered where to turn for a roommate, Bailey had found herself constrained in an unfamiliar way. In the past, moving in with friends had been a simple matter of finding out who had an extra bedroom. Now she had to consider what might happen five months from now when she gave birth. And she might be putting a friend in an awkward position.

Take Ned. He was Owen's nurse. How unfair to ask him such a favor when the result might be tension at work. She couldn't query a casual acquaintance like Erica, whose first loyalty was to Owen, while many other friends like Patty and Nora were now married or engaged.

At lunch, Bailey had checked bulletin boards in the nurses' lounges, only to catch a couple of women regarding her with a mixture of curiosity and something that made her squirm. It was the fascinated horror with which people stared at celebrities who got into trouble.

She'd fled into the corridor, where she ran into Renée, who was pushing an empty wheelchair toward a patient's room. When the older woman stopped to talk, Bailey blurted her dilemma about finding a place to stay. Renée immediately volunteered her spare bedroom.

"I can't promise anything permanent," the older woman had said. "I'm a bit set in my ways and, as you'll see, my house is stuffed with my own possessions. But there's room in the garage to store your things and I'd love to have you there for however long it takes you to find the right place."

"That could be a few months," Bailey had warned.

"No problem." Renée beamed at her. "It'll be fun to share such an exciting time with you. And I do get lonely. Having a guest for a few weeks or months ought to be a nice change."

In response to the word *guest,* Bailey had insisted on paying rent. Reluctantly, Renée had named a modest amount that wouldn't do much more than repay her for extra utilities and other costs. Bailey had agreed with gratitude.

Ned and some of the other male nurses had helped move her stuff into Renée's garage. She'd thanked everyone by buying take-out, after which she and Renée had discovered they shared an affection for old TV sitcoms.

But Bailey never forgot that Renée had once faced a dilemma somewhat like hers. Pregnant and on her own, she'd given up a baby. That didn't explain why she'd never had other children.

"Didn't your husband want children?" Bailey prompted. Her hostess seemed lost in memories.

"He had no strong feelings either way, peculiar as that might sound." Renée's gaze remained dreamy. "He was older than me and had never married before. In fact, he'd lived with his mother until she died. I don't think he felt comfortable around kids."

Bailey recalled that the man had died two years ago. Judging by how thoroughly Renée had settled into this house, they'd probably lived here together. "He didn't mind all the figurines and stuff?"

Her friend chuckled. "You're going to think me strange, but this house belonged to his mother and so did a lot of the knickknacks. I already had a small collection of my own and they blended right in. Please don't read anything psychological into it. I was *not* a substitute for Hubert's mother, believe me."

Bailey hadn't been thinking that. "The house is not exactly a kid-friendly place. You'd have had to pack away this breakable stuff."

"True." Renée straightened the lace doily on her chair's arm. "We quit using birth control for a while, but nothing happened. We had to decide whether to consult a doctor, adopt or accept whatever nature did or didn't send us. We went with option three, and that was that."

"I'm sorry," Bailey said.

"Hubert and I had a happy marriage for nearly thirty years. If I had children, that would be wonderful for me now, but I'm not so sure it would have been good for the two of us."

Thirty years together. She couldn't imagine being so lucky. "I wonder if I'll ever meet a man like Hubert."

Renée hesitated for a moment before asking, "You aren't involved with Dr. Tartikoff? Or is that too personal a question?"

Bailey didn't blame her for wondering. "According to him, we aren't involved, so there you have it."

"His loss."

Bailey stretched. "Is there anything in that cute pig-shaped cookie jar in the kitchen or is that just for decoration?"

Renée laughed. "I love baking cookies. I keep them around for my neighbors' children and, yes, I'd be happy to share."

"You're the perfect roommate," Bailey told her as they got up.

"I've missed having someone to mother," was the cheerful response.

Later, drifting off in the canopied guest bed, Bailey thought about the decision she had to face. What a wonderful fantasy, to keep her two little angels and watch them grow into healthy toddlers, but how unrealistic. She'd lucked out today thanks to Renée's generosity, but when it came to finding a new home big enough for the three of them, there was no fallback position.

Phyllis and Boone had left her with no savings. Worse, the one relative she'd always figured she could count on in a crisis—her sister—had turned against her. Yes, some single moms succeeded in raising kids on their own. If there were only one baby...if she had more money...if Owen loved her...

Her chest squeezed. But he didn't. More and more, the choice seemed inevitable. She had to find the babies a stable home where they could grow up with loving, committed parents.

No sooner would she say hello than she'd have to say goodbye.

Her hand pressing her abdomen, Bailey whispered, "Forgive me." And felt the pillow grow damp with the tears she'd been holding back.

Chapter Seventeen

During the next month, Owen developed a strong empathy for tightrope walkers, especially those who balanced poles, juggled plates and performed other amazing feats in midair. The hospital went ahead full speed with plans to unveil the fertility program to the public, which meant that in addition to maintaining his schedule of performing surgery, seeing patients and hiring key employees, he had to be available for numerous special events. By the time he got home to bed, he often could scarcely remember what day it was.

Also, he couldn't ignore the unfolding criminal case against his brother. More evidence came to light of Boone's international wheelings and dealings, and by now it was well established, at least in the public's mind, that there'd never been any intent to invest the money. It was all one big scam.

As for Phyllis, he gathered from TV that his sister-in-law was cooperating fully with the authorities. To the media, she positioned herself as the abandoned, overly trusting spouse, and while Owen didn't believe that absolved her of all blame, he had to admit she'd been played for a fool like everyone else. Thanks to the information she'd provided, about a quarter of the stolen money had been recovered, but prosecutors warned that the rest might be gone forever, stashed in secret bank accounts or safe deposit boxes that Boone hoped someday to retrieve.

Bailey's initiative in moving out of the house had helped defuse reporters' interest in Owen. While unpleasant insinuations and inappropriate questions occasionally popped up during the grand opening, they became less frequent. Owen's ready availability helped defuse matters, since he was obviously not trying to hide anything.

Ironically, in focusing international attention on Safe Harbor, the stir about Boone benefited the program's debut. The outstanding facilities, the excellent staff—except for a head of the men's fertility program, a position he still hadn't filled—and advance word of an innovative surgical technique that Owen was set to describe next month at a major conference got far more air time than anyone had anticipated.

It was a good thing he had a lot of balls to juggle, because he found it uncomfortable to linger at home. The place felt wrong without Bailey. He would open the refrigerator expecting to swipe one of her yogurts before he remembered she didn't live here anymore. Or hurry into the bathroom only to see the counter nearly empty and realize no one was going to push his stuff aside and drive him crazy. No one set up a keyboard on the dining table, or played havoc with his laundry, or poked him in the ego when he needed it.

His repeated calls to her cell phone went straight to voice mail. He kept the messages succinct. "Do you need anything? Please let me know." And "I have to make sure you and the twins are okay. Call me." She didn't. He stooped to querying Ned, who explained that she was staying with an older friend and that everything appeared to be fine. Owen didn't probe further. He had no right to put his nurse in the middle.

He did hear that she'd begun receiving prenatal care from Dr. Sargent, but since both his and Nora's offices were a floor below Owen's, he had little chance of running into Bailey in the hall. A vague hope of encountering her in the elevator failed to materialize, and when he did catch sight of her across the lobby, she always hurried off. He could hardly chase her down in full public view and demand that she talk to him.

Well, they had time. The twins weren't due until January, and while they might arrive a month early, that was still in the future. As for this ache inside, this void where Bailey ought to be, Owen knew he'd better come up with a plan, but so far he hadn't had a spare moment to think of one.

By the end of September, with the grand opening over, the open houses and celebrity visits and other events finally wound down. Late one Monday afternoon, Ned went around the office glumly tossing out wilting bouquets and fading decorations. "What a letdown," he grumbled.

Owen, who'd been catching up on paperwork after seeing his last patient of the day, regarded the usually cheerful young man in surprise. "I can order more flowers if that'll float your boat," he said.

"No, thanks." The nurse leaned against a counter. "It isn't just me. Everybody feels it. I mean, the opening's been this great success but now it's back to work as usual."

While Owen didn't share the sense of anticlimax, since he was preparing for next month's conference in L.A., he had to admit he'd noticed a lack of zip in other staff members these past few days. Not much he could do about that, but he could cheer up his hardworking assistant. "You've been with me how long now, six weeks?"

Ned gave a nod, his expression cautious. He'd lost some of his tan, which probably meant the guy hadn't been spending as much time as usual at the beach. No wonder. He'd worked hard at reorganizing the office.

"Well, there's no reason to wait out the full three-month trial period," Owen went on. "Your position here is permanent, if you want it to be." The spontaneous decision felt right.

Those blue eyes lit up. "That's great! I...thanks, Dr. T." That was the nickname most of the staff used these days.

"You earned it."

They were shaking hands when Caroline poked her head out of the reception area. "There's someone here to see you, Dr. T."

"There's no one on the schedule," Ned responded protectively.

"She's not here for a checkup. She says she's a former patient."

Owen saw no reason to stand on ceremony. Heading for the waiting room, he asked, "What's her name?"

"Trish Royce."

That rang a bell. A prominent banking executive in Boston, Mrs. Royce had waited until she was nearly forty to start a family, then failed to conceive after more than a year. While other doctors had suggested halfway measures, Owen had looked at her test results and told her frankly that her eggs weren't viable.

"If you want to bear a child, you'll need donor eggs." He'd seen the pain in her face, but delaying would only make matters worse. "We can use your husband's sperm, and your chances of carrying a child look good at this point. I'd advise moving forward quickly. Time is not your friend."

"You're awfully blunt." A tall woman in a designer suit, she'd wrapped her arms around herself. Her husband had asked a couple of questions, and Owen had explained his reasoning in detail. By the end of that first visit, the Royces had agreed to go with a donor.

A little over a year later, she'd given birth to fraternal twin sons. She'd sent Owen a photo and a thank-you note afterward, and that was the last he'd heard from her.

In the front room, he had to admit he wouldn't have recognized the woman sitting on the floor racing toy cars with two boys. Instead of a suit, she wore pants and a flowing woven top, and she was making vroom-vroom noises as if she, too, were a kid.

"Oh! I didn't expect you to come out so quickly." Jumping to her feet, she gave Owen a grin. "I wasn't sure if you'd remember me."

"Sure I do." Intrigued, Owen shook hands and then examined the two lively faces much like their mother's. No one would imagine that they weren't genetically related. "What terrific young men. To what do I owe the honor of this visit?"

"My husband and I are living out here now. I keep seeing you on the news and I couldn't resist dropping by." Trish gave a happy shrug. "I guess moms bring their kids to visit all the time."

"Infants, occasionally, but not at this age. They're how old—five?"

"And three months."

Owen noted an open bag on one of the couches, with picture books spilling out. "I can see you keep them busy."

"Billy's starting to read already, and he's teaching his brother," Trish said.

"Teaching his brother?" That was unusual.

"Jim's more into visuals. He likes to sketch. Billy's a word person. He's been encouraging his brother to draw pictures to go with the sounds of letters. Can you believe that? Their kindergarten teacher said she's never seen anything like it." Trish had gained a few pounds along with some wrinkles around the eyes, but to Owen she seemed radiant. "If you hadn't given me that push, I doubt I'd have them. And they're such a miracle."

"They certainly are." Had it really been five years since their birth? If Owen had given the matter any thought, he'd have visualized them as toddlers. "They grow up fast."

"You're the one who emphasized how quickly things change," Trish reminded him. "I had this image of myself as a young woman, and it wasn't pleasant at first, realizing that to you I was nearly over the hill."

"I wouldn't put it that way, but we have to be realistic." Owen didn't waste time on complimenting his patients; they came to him for help, not flattery. "Although women are having babies later these days, there are a lot of questions about the health implications." He'd heard of a Spanish woman who gave birth, amid plenty of controversy, at the age of sixty-seven. Tragically, she'd died two years later.

"I appreciated your honesty," Trish continued. "So, speaking of time passing, do you have kids of your own by now?"

She had no way of knowing what a loaded question that was. "Not yet," Owen said.

"I guess it's different for men, but don't wait too long, Doc," Trish advised with a wink.

"Good advice." Owen spent a few more minutes catching up on her activities and the twins' development. The happy mother gave him a hug and he couldn't resist squatting to give the boys one as well. After only a moment's hesitation, Billy flung his arms around Owen, totally fearless. When it was Jim's turn, the little boy stood back, thrust out a hand and shook solemnly. "They really are different," Owen observed, straightening.

"Utterly," Trish said. "Once you have kids, you'll understand."

His chest tightened. Somehow, Owen managed to say goodbye in a pleasant manner, but his brain was working feverishly.

No one knew that Bailey's twins were his. Nor, as a donor, did he have any legal rights. Why had he assumed she would simply carry on until they were born without making plans? She could hand them over to Phyllis, or do something really crazy like marry a guy she didn't love for security.

What about this friend she was staying with? Male or female?

Agitated, he went in search of Ned. But it was after five o'clock, and he discovered the nurse had left, no doubt to celebrate his good news. Caroline was gone also, not that he'd have trusted her enough to ask such a leading question. To his knowledge she hadn't done any more gossiping, but Owen preferred to play it safe.

He locked the office and took the elevator down. It stopped at the second floor.

When the doors opened, Bailey's moss-green eyes widened in something close to alarm. He felt a rush of joy at the sight of that familiar face, but for a moment, he feared she might refuse to get in.

"Oh, come on. Live dangerously," Owen said. *Give me a chance to tease you out of this mood.*

Bailey stalked forward, turned and faced front. "Are you sure it's safe to be seen with me?"

"Don't be petty." Owen couldn't afford to waste time arguing. The elevator was moving again, and he had questions to ask. "How are you?"

"Dr. Sargent says everything's fine."

"I didn't mean that. Well, not entirely." Slight thump,

and the doors parted. Had they reached the first floor already? "I'll walk you to your car."

She narrowed her eyes at him, but didn't object, perhaps because the lobby was bustling with people emerging from the other elevator and the ground-floor hallways. It wasn't Bailey's style to make a scene, thank goodness.

Outside, chrysanthemums bloomed by the walkway and the mild September air smelled of brine. Noticing the roughness of the sidewalk, Owen took Bailey's arm. "Can't have you stumbling," he said when she stiffened.

"Is there something you want?" she asked.

"I want to know why you're mad at me and why you won't return my phone calls." He should have stopped there, but the questions kept coming. "Also this friend you're staying with. Is it a healthy situation? I mean, is this a person you can trust? Honestly, there's no reason you can't move back into the house."

"You're not embarrassed if people find out?"

"I was never embarrassed. It was simply an awkward situation that could have damaged both of our reputations and the hospital's." Owen slowed his pace to match hers. She had short legs, and her midsection had grown dramatically this past month. "Can you feel the babies moving?"

"All the time," she said, still not meeting his gaze.

Their children were growing. He'd missed so much. The month had been busy, productive, important. But he'd never get back those evenings when he might have been sitting beside Bailey, his hand on her abdomen, registering the changes in the babies.

"Phyllis isn't still pressuring you to give them up, is she?" he asked.

"She's called a few times. She can be sweet, and she can be nasty. I don't trust her." Bailey sounded miserable. "She's the one person I always thought I could count on."

"You can count on me," he blurted.

"To do what?" Bailey snapped. "Let me move back into the house? If people thought it was strange before, they'd really gossip now. You may be the babies' uncle, as far as they're concerned, but since Phyllis is talking about divorcing your brother, we won't even be related much longer."

He hadn't thought of that. "We'll always have a connection."

"I'm going to give them up for adoption," Bailey said. "It's the best thing for everyone."

Give them up? Owen halted at the entrance to the parking garage. "You can't do that."

"Do the words *watch me* mean anything to you?"

"I'm the father."

"Say it a little louder," Bailey told him. "Someone might hear. But we can't have that, can we?"

Why not? Owen caught his breath. He felt as if a thousand longings were colliding in his brain. He needed a chance to sort them out.

Bailey removed her arm from his grasp. "If this is guilt speaking, don't worry about me. Owen, I never expected anything from you. I know I'm not your kind of woman."

That was news to him. "Whatever gave you that idea?"

"I heard about the women you dated in Boston—they were as different from me as you can get," Bailey said. "And I accept that you're not the kind of guy who sticks around. Well, maybe with someone who thinks like you and flies up there in the stratosphere with you. Anyway, I don't need your pity."

"Pity is the furthest thing from my mind." He didn't have a name for this welter of feelings: desire and tenderness mixed with an almost overwhelming urge to stand guard over her. If only she'd slow down and give him a minute. Usually, Owen's brain worked faster than everyone else's, but he was in unfamiliar territory here.

"Get on with your life and I'll handle mine." Did Bailey realize her quivering chin gave her away? "This is my problem and I'm dealing with it." With that, she swung around and headed into the parking structure.

"We aren't finished," Owen said.

She merely waggled one hand in the air. He considered going after her, but then his phone rang. Much as Owen would have liked to ignore it, he couldn't risk leaving one of his surgical patients in a crisis. "Yes?"

It was Alec Denny. As Owen listened to his friend's unexpected announcement, he watched Bailey cross paths with another pregnant woman who was holding hands with a man. The couple moved on, leaving Bailey's solitary figure to proceed alone.

It gave him an idea. Or at least the beginning of one.

Chapter Eighteen

On the drive home, Bailey replayed the conversation with multiple variations. In some versions, she railed at Owen for breaking her heart, which she was very glad she hadn't done. In others, she left out the stuff about the women in Boston because that made her sound as if she were jealous. Sometimes she emphasized that these were *his* babies and watched him gaze at her with melting adoration, which he obviously hadn't done. In her opinion, Owen Tartikoff wasn't capable of melting adoration.

None of the adaptations came out to her satisfaction, because she'd have liked to see him abjectly remorseful and hopelessly in love with her, which was impossible. She couldn't picture him ever, under any circumstances, presenting her to the high-and-mighty physicians of Safe Harbor as the future Mrs. Tartikoff. Let alone revealing to anyone, even his closest friends, that he was the father of her children.

Bailey had spent much of her fantasy life believing in fairy tales. Then she'd had to go and fall for the ogre. Typical.

At the cottage, she found a cheerful Renée taking a lasagna out of the oven. During the past month, her hostess had rediscovered a love of cooking, now that she had someone to appreciate the results. "I'm sure I'll get tired of it eventually," Renée had warned, "but let's both enjoy it while it lasts."

Determinedly, Bailey pushed Owen from her thoughts and settled down to the meal. While she did share a lot of her feelings with Renée, she hadn't talked much about Dr. T. Too sensitive a subject. Mostly, they discussed the hospital, Phyllis, Boone and the babies.

At six, Renée switched on a small set she kept in the kitchen. They both liked watching local news.

After the latest regional highlights, the newscaster said, "Exclusive interview with Phyllis Storey, right after the break. You won't want to miss her surprise declaration. Stay tuned!"

Renée muted the ensuing commercial. "Do you suppose she filed for divorce?"

"How would that surprise anyone?" Bailey asked.

"They have to promote some angle. To keep suckers like us watching."

Bailey wished her sister didn't relish the limelight so much. No telling what she'd say just to stay the center of attention.

A minute later, the newscast returned. There sat Phyllis, her hair color brightened to a honey-blonde. "You said you're going public with a personal matter," the anchor-woman prompted.

"That's right, Lacey." Phyllis swung toward the camera. "Before all this ugliness with my husband came crashing down, my sister agreed to serve as a surrogate mother for Boone and me. I was overjoyed when we learned she was carrying twins."

"She should shut up now," Bailey said.

"Agreed." But Renée made no move to turn off the TV, and Bailey didn't ask her to.

On-screen, the anchorwoman prompted, "There's nothing wrong with the babies, I hope."

Phyllis's jaw took on a bulldog tightness. If only there were some way to reach out and shake her before she spoke again.

Too late. "As a result of my husband's wrongdoing, Bailey backed out on our deal. She refuses to hand over the babies." Phyllis made it sound as if they'd already been born.

"But surely you have legal rights."

Phyllis gazed pleadingly at the camera. "I'm afraid not. You see, they're her eggs, so I don't have any rights. I can't tell you what a betrayal this is. I practically raised my sister, who's twelve years younger than me. She can have lots of children, but I can't, and she knows it. I'm an experienced mother, old enough to understand their needs. She's just being selfish and vindictive because she invested some of her money with Boone."

"Some?" Bailey demanded of the screen. "You mean *all!*"

"Aren't you going to take legal action?" prompted the interviewer.

"What's that woman trying to do?" Renée snarled.

Phyllis made a fluttery gesture. "You can't sue someone for being disloyal. I just want to issue a plea to my sister. Think about those helpless little infants and what their lives will be like with a mother who never wanted them or planned for them."

It was the anchorwoman's turn to face the camera. "There you are, folks. If Bailey Storey is listening to this broadcast…"

"Bailey Wayne," Phyllis corrected.

"I appeal to her to join us. Let us hear your side of the

story. Now, let's check out the latest on that fire burning in Riverside County…"

Renée clicked off the set. "Maybe you ought to go on the air and let everyone know how your sister dropped the ball on paying for your medical care."

"She'd twist whatever I said to position herself as a victim." Bailey could imagine Phyllis replaying the painful details of her miscarriages. "I just hope people at the hospital don't pay attention to this."

"I'll set them straight if they do," Renée promised. "Maybe I don't have a lot of clout as a volunteer, but I can speak my mind."

"I appreciate it." As Bailey cleared the dishes, she had to admit that to the casual observer, her decision to back out of the surrogacy agreement must look bad. It would be different if people knew all the financial details and especially that Boone wasn't the father, but revealing the truth would hurt Owen. How ironic that Phyllis had accused her of disloyalty when she was loyal to a fault…to a man who might never appreciate it.

Bailey's cell rang. "That better not be Phyllis." She dug it from her pocket. "Hello?"

"Hey, Bailey." Patty's upbeat voice had an immediate calming event. "Hope you're not busy next Saturday."

Quick mental check. She wasn't expected at the counseling clinic and hadn't made any other plans. "Don't think so. What's up?"

"Alec says the staff's bummed now that the opening's finished, so we decided to throw our wedding at the hospital. Kind of a boost to morale."

"You're scheduling your wedding to cheer up the staff?" That was unusual enough, and then the timing struck Bailey. "This Saturday? Patty, nobody puts together a wedding that fast."

She could picture her friend's honest gray eyes blinking away the objection. "Oh, hey, no problem. Jennifer Martin is decorating the auditorium and the cafeteria's going to cater. I insisted on a big stack of bear claws instead of a wedding cake."

"Okay, you're officially nuts, but what about your dress?"

"My mother-in-law is in charge of costumes," Patty said blithely. "Here's the thing. I'm stuck having my wacko sister, Rainbow, as my maid of honor, but I want you to be my bridesmaid."

"You haven't seen me lately," Bailey protested. "I'm as round as a beach ball."

"Who cares? Fiona's the flower girl and she's scared to walk up an aisle in front of all those people." Alec's five-year-old daughter was a real cutie. "She asked if you'd walk with her."

"Why me?" A few months ago, Bailey had worn her nurse's uniform to help run a teddy bear clinic at Fiona's birthday party. They'd spent a delightful few hours bandaging stuffed animals and taking their vital signs, but she hadn't seen the little girl since then.

"She watched a movie where somebody fainted during a wedding and she insists we need Nurse Bailey on hand," Patty said. "I explained that the hospital's full of medical personnel, especially with Owen being the best man—"

"Owen's the best man?" That could be awkward.

"It's important that my stepdaughter enjoy the wedding. I'm counting on you. Say yes, okay?"

She might as well. Bailey wouldn't miss Patty's wedding for anything, and she didn't want to hurt Fiona's feelings. "Sure. What should I wear?"

"Darlene will be in touch. Like I said, she's handling the clothes. Frankly, I'd be happy to wear my tuxedo but she put her foot down." At Nora's wedding in May, Patty had worn a tux to stand up as best man for Leo, who'd been her patrol partner at the police department before she left to become a detective. The outfit suited her, in Bailey's opinion, but didn't every little girl dream of a white dress with lots of lace?

"We'll have a run-through Saturday morning and the big event's at three," Patty finished. "The whole staff's invited and that includes your friend Renée. Let her know, will you? We aren't exactly sending formal invitations. More of a blanket email."

"You bet."

Smiling, Bailey clicked off. Patty was right. The idea of a wedding did boost her spirits. It was great to have something to look forward to.

THAT WEEK, BAILEY CLUNG TO her sense of anticipation. She needed it to counteract the annoyance when Phyllis went on the air again, pleading her case as a mom with a broken heart. She must have given the TV station Bailey's cell number, because a woman called several times, trying to persuade her to let them tape an interview. Bailey refused.

On the wedding front, Alec's mother, Darlene Denny, took Bailey shopping and showed her a photo of Patty's sister, Rainbow, an ethereal young woman with flowing blond hair dyed with a pink streak. She was wearing the lavender bridesmaid dress she'd chosen. That shade of pale purple turned Bailey's skin ashen.

"Ever heard of the movie *Corpse Bride?*" she grumbled to Darlene. "Well, I'll be the corpse bridesmaid."

"We don't have to go all matchy-matchy," the older woman assured her. "Fiona plans to wear pink. Let's see what we can scare up for you in a complementary shade."

They found a maternity dress in deep rose that flattered

Bailey's coloring and coordinated with Fi's outfit. Darlene insisted the bridal couple pay for it. Bailey would have objected, but she couldn't afford to. Since Phyllis hadn't bought her any maternity outfits, Bailey had been shopping for them at secondhand stores.

At work, she'd started bringing her lunch to eat in the office because walking through the cafeteria became an ordeal. While her friends stood by her, there were plenty of near-strangers who seemed to have nothing better to do than gossip. On Tuesday, she caught the words *selfish* and *probably go on welfare,* and only resisted dumping her lunch tray on the offending loudmouth because she didn't want to waste the food.

There were no further calls from Owen. Several times in the medical building, she caught him staring at her, but did her best to ignore him. The guy had no idea how much she was sacrificing to protect his secret.

Bailey hadn't yet had the heart to talk to a counselor about adoption. Once she chose a couple, she supposed they might help her financially, but she'd have to stop thinking of the babies as hers. And she wasn't ready to do that.

The scorching hot end-of-September weather cooled off by Friday. Bailey's temper didn't, however, because the evening newscast featured a panel discussion with a medical ethicist, a former surrogate and a woman who claimed to be an advocate for the rights of parents who hired surrogates. Despite a strong urge to turn them off, she watched out of self-defense. Their theme was pretty much what Phyllis had been saying—a deal was a deal.

Yes, in Bailey's opinion, it should be. But she wasn't the one who'd broken faith.

"You should fight back," Renée urged.

"Maybe next week." She had no idea what she'd say, though.

That night, Bailey cried herself to sleep. How had her life turned into such a mess, when all she'd tried to do was help her sister? Instead, she'd been made a public pariah, become mother to two babies she couldn't keep and fallen in love with a guy who was rapidly forgetting she existed.

BY SATURDAY MORNING, the steeply raked wood-paneled auditorium had been transformed with a profusion of pink, lavender and white flowers and ribbons. Darlene had arranged for the minister from her church to preside, and someone had set up a handsome piano beside the on-stage altar.

The rehearsal went off smoothly except for Fiona dropping her bouquet, which Bailey assured her was good luck. As for Bailey herself, she felt a touch nervous, but that was probably because of the way Owen kept sneaking glances at her.

What did the man expect her to do? She wasn't going to move back into the house just to keep him company.

That afternoon, Bailey joined Patty in Alec's fifth-floor office to help the bride change into her gown. Jennifer had set up a portable full-length mirror, where Patty examined herself skeptically.

"What a gorgeous dress. It fits you perfectly." Bailey meant every word.

"It's rented." Patty ran a brush through her straight, chin-length blond hair and replaced the circlet of flowers she'd chosen in lieu of a hat or veil. She—or more likely Darlene—had chosen an elegant long gown with lace covering the shoulders and arms. No strapless design for this bride. "Can't see spending that much money on a dress I'm only going to wear once."

"You could wear it again to renew your vows on your tenth or twentieth anniversary." Bailey had read about such ceremonies in the newspaper, although she didn't personally know anyone whose marriage had lasted that long. Certainly not in her family.

Patty shrugged. "Why do I need to renew my vows? I don't plan to break them. Oh, hey, look who just showed up."

In sashayed Rainbow, who bore little resemblance to her older, taller sister. Her dreamy air gave the impression she'd just materialized from another plane of existence. An employee at a bookstore in San Francisco, Rainbow had grown up with their ex-hippie parents in Arizona, while Patty and her brother had been raised by their strict, ex-military grandfather here in Safe Harbor.

"Is she here yet?" Rainbow asked, which seemed a strange question with the bride standing right in front of her. "I think that's so romantic the way—"

"You are *not* wearing flip-flops at my wedding." Patty glowered at her sister.

"What? Oh." Rainbow regarded her feet as if she'd never seen them before. "I've got pumps in my bag."

"And your bag is where?"

"Uh. In my car." Off she went.

"Let's hope she doesn't disappear. She vanished for five hours on Friday to go to Disneyland, only she didn't tell anybody." The amusement park was about half an hour's drive to the north. "Fiona was bummed that her new aunt didn't take her along, but I wouldn't trust Rainbow with my daughter."

"What was she talking about?" Bailey asked. "Is there someone else in the ceremony?"

Patty blinked. "Who else would be in the ceremony?" She recalled the piano. "A singer?"

"You should dismiss anything Rainbow tells you unless it's supported by a notarized document," Patty responded. "Maybe she meant Fi. She and Darlene are meeting us downstairs. I hope my sister has the sense to do the same."

"Things will come together," Bailey assured her.

Patty glanced at an overhead clock. "Time to go down. Let's get this show on the road."

And quite a show it was, Bailey noted as they made their way out of the suite and along the hallway to the elevator. Patients out for a stroll from rooms in an adjoining corridor smiled and gave Patty thumbs-up, while nurses exclaimed over the dress. A couple of them regarded Bailey with dubious expressions. Recognizing the loudmouth from the cafeteria, Bailey pointedly ignored her.

Unfortunately, their presence served as a reminder that Bailey was about to march down an aisle in front of half the staff. That reflection dimmed some of the pleasure she took in helping Patty lift her skirt off the elevator floor and seeing the bemused reactions of passersby when they reached the ground level.

"Bailey! Bailey!" Up scampered a delightful little girl in a fluffy pink dress. With her brown hair cut like Patty's and a matching circlet of flowers atop her head, Fiona was too precious for words.

"How's our flower girl?" Bailey gave the little girl a careful hug.

"Pretty dress," the child pronounced, examining Bailey's finery. "But not as pretty as my new mom's!" A powerful bond had already formed between Patty and Fi. Although Alec's self-absorbed first wife was entitled to visit their daughter, she hadn't showed up in months, Patty had mentioned.

If I had a little girl, I'd spend every possible minute with her. Except, Bailey reflected with a twist of sorrow, she *did* have a little girl and a boy, too, and she couldn't afford to keep them.

"You both look beautiful," agreed Darlene, a slender woman in her late-fifties.

"Thanks."

Rainbow joined them, her flip-flops replaced by ridiculously high, sparkly wedges. "I'm here!"

"Welcome back," Patty said.

Their brother, Drew, handsome in his army uniform, came to escort Darlene to her seat and then returned to accompany his sister. As planned, the bridal party gathered in a small room near the auditorium, out of sight until Jennifer cued them.

"Everybody's seated," the PR director announced. "Oh, my, don't you all look gorgeous! Are you nervous?"

"Me?" Patty said. "Yeah, I'm afraid I'll fall off these heels."

Rainbow glanced at her feet. "They're about two inches high."

"That's two inches higher than nature intended," her sister shot back.

Jennifer peered into the hall. "Coast's clear. Let's go."

They billowed out in their finery. Jennifer stuck her head into the auditorium to cue the pianist, and the music shifted into the melody that signaled the beginning of the wedding march. With a radiant smile plastered on her face, Rainbow disappeared through the door Jennifer held ajar.

"One down," Patty said.

"Bailey!" cried Fiona with sudden fright.

"What, sweetie?"

"What if I trip?"

Bailey reached for her hand. "I'll hold you."

"What if I drop the flowers?"

"That's good luck, remember? But only if it's an accident," she added as a precaution.

"Promise you'll hold on to me?"

"I promise," she said, suffused with tenderness.

Peering down into Fiona's trusting brown eyes, Bailey felt an overwhelming rush of emotion. Who was going to be holding her children's hands for all those years ahead? What if they were alone or frightened and there was no one to reassure and protect them?

Someday, they'll be walking down the aisles at their own weddings, but I won't be there. I'll never see what kind of people they've grown up to become or whether I made the right decision.

She couldn't bear not knowing whether they were safe and loved. She had to be there for them.

No matter what it cost or how much she had to sacrifice, she couldn't give them up.

Chapter Nineteen

Jennifer gestured urgently. "Now, now!"

Embarrassed to have missed her cue, Bailey took a firm grip on Fiona's hand and started forward. The door parted, and in they went.

The place was packed. Stifling a rush of panic, Bailey registered the faces of administrators, doctors, nurses, support staff, volunteers, all focused on her and Fiona. But they were safe, holding each other's hands, and as the little girl proceeded solemnly forward, smiles bloomed in their direction.

Finally Bailey dared to glance ahead to the altar set up on the stage, and the two men standing there. Alec Denny, face alight with love, and Owen.

She'd never seen a man look so thoroughly masculine in a tuxedo. Against the severe black and white, he was like a flame with his russet hair and the intensity of his gaze. Oddly, she caught a flicker of uncertainty in his expression, and his mouth parted as if to frame a question.

For a moment, there was no one else in the auditorium. Only Owen, fixing her in the spotlight of his gaze.

Then she and Fi reached the low steps and climbed up. "Way to go!" whispered Rainbow as Bailey guided Fiona into position next to the maid of honor.

The music transitioned to the formal wedding march.

Amid the rustles and sighs that greeted the sight of the bride, she caught a few low whistles and mutterings of "Go, Patty!" Ah, yes. Among the hospital personnel Bailey recognized a sprinkling of the bride's old buddies from the police department.

Only her brother's measured pace kept Patty from galloping down the aisle, but in due time, he handed her over.

Patty glowed as she regarded her groom. "Hey."

"Hey, back," Alec murmured happily, and pulled her into place beside him.

Beautiful as the ceremony was, Bailey found it hard to concentrate. She was too aware of Owen studying her—didn't he realize everyone could see?—and of the implications of the emotional commitment she'd just made to the twins. It ran soul-deep, this love of her children that she'd tried so hard to dismiss. Maybe she'd regret this, she told herself. Maybe someday she'd discover how much she'd deprived them of, growing up with little money and no father, just as she had. Maybe, as Phyllis said, she was being selfish—although not for keeping them from her irresponsible, manipulative sister.

Would Owen ever visit them? Would they have red hair like his? Would anyone guess that they were related?

Bailey blinked away tears. She'd always known that whatever man stole her heart would leave a void behind. At least she had two angelic babies and a heart full of love to fill that emptiness.

Almost.

The sound of the minister introducing the newly wedded couple to their guests jolted Bailey from her reverie. Applause rang out, and into the aisle went the happy duo, arm in arm, with Rainbow and Fiona practically skipping behind. Weighed down, Bailey had to hurry to keep up.

She felt like a huge tortoise, waddling after them all by herself.

Wait a minute. Why was Owen still standing near the altar?

He held up his hands, quieting the crowd. "If you folks will bear with me for a moment, there's a little more entertainment before you get to eat. Delicious as that cafeteria food is, I'm hoping you'll indulge me."

A scattering of laughter greeted this remark, and those who'd stood up sank into their seats again. Uncertainly, Bailey retreated toward the exit. Whatever fun and games Owen had in mind, she wasn't in the mood.

"Whoa." Bouquet raised, Patty blocked her path. "Don't make me tackle you. It'll look really weird with me wearing this fancy dress and you being pregnant and all."

"What's going on?"

"You'll see."

Puzzled, Bailey turned to face the stage. Owen, who'd taken a position next to the piano, was watching her with an unaccustomed air of vulnerability. What on earth did he plan to do?

The moment the pianist hit the opening chord, she recognized the melody. Out of all the songs Rodgers and Hammerstein ever wrote, this was her favorite, the most beautiful, the most heartfelt, the most inspiring.

And Owen was singing it directly to her. As if he didn't care that half the hospital was watching. That word might leak out to the press. That people might scoff.

Overwhelmed, Bailey sank into an empty seat and got lost in the beauty of "You'll Never Walk Alone."

No matter what life brought, no matter how dark the storm, there'd always be a light at the end. If only it were true. If only he meant it. But you couldn't trust hope. It squeezed your heart and made you imagine possibilities that would never come true. Not for you.

When his rich voice finished and the last chord died away, applause rocked the auditorium. Bailey heard cheers, most loudly from Patty and Alec. But of course this tribute was meant for them. How appropriate.

Owen had his hands up for silence again. When it fell, he cleared his throat. "Just one more thing. Begging your patience, folks. I've had a hard time getting a word in with Miss Bailey Wayne recently, so please forgive my taking advantage of this occasion. I assure you, I cleared it with the bride and groom first."

What was he doing? Around the room, Bailey heard a stir of anticipation.

"There's been an unfair rumor going around that Bailey's just a surrogate who stole her sister and brother-in-law's children." Now Owen had the audience's full attention. "Well, her sister tricked and lied to her. You see, my brother may be fertile when it comes to hatching plots, but not when it comes to fatherhood."

Bailey's jaw dropped. Was he really going to say this in front of everyone?

"I made a very personal donation to help *my* brother and sister-in-law have kids. But they deceived both Bailey and me. I didn't know there was a surrogate, and she didn't know that those babies she's carrying are mine."

A gasp skittered throughout the room. Even Patty and Alec were staring at him in shock. Apparently he hadn't told them this part.

Which part *had* he told them?

Owen soldiered on. "They also broke their promise to pay for Bailey's medical care. Instead, they gave her a place to live in what just happened to be the other half of my house. Then a funny thing happened."

His gaze fixed on Bailey. She couldn't have looked away if a bomb had gone off.

"You see, I fell in love with the lady, and I don't like seeing her walk alone," Owen said. "I think she should have someone by her side for, say, the rest of her life, and I think our children should grow up with two loving parents. Bailey Wayne, will you marry me?"

Around her, the auditorium had gone completely still. Staring at the man she loved through the flowers and ribbons, she asked the first question that popped into her mind. "You mean right now?"

He grinned, and she heard a few sympathetic chuckles in the audience. "Any time you want, sweetheart, although I was hoping to wait until we got a marriage license and a ring. Oh, wait." He patted his pocket. "Already took care of that part."

Then he did the second most amazing thing Bailey had ever seen. He descended the steps, took out a jeweler's box and opened it to display a diamond ring that glowed almost as brightly as his eyes.

Right there in the aisle, in front of everyone, he got down on one knee. And the great Dr. Tartikoff proposed all over again.

Fiona, who'd been fidgeting on the sidelines, could contain herself no longer. "Say yes!"

Bailey's cheeks burned. Leaning close to Owen, drinking in his very male scent, she felt his hair tickle her nose as she whispered, "Yes."

His face lit with happiness. "You better mean that," he whispered back.

"I promise," she said.

He slipped the ring onto her finger, and then he kissed her hand. Around them, a cheer went up, with Patty yelling louder than anyone. "Yay for Bailey and Owen! Hurrah!"

As he helped Bailey to her feet, she was amazed to see the number of people hurrying toward them, laughing and calling out congratulations. Renée, of course, and Ned, who started pumping Owen's hand as if trying to draw water from a well. Nora and her husband, Lori and Devina and Caroline, Dr. Rayburn, Dr. Forrest, Dr. Sargent and all sorts of other people crowded around. She'd had no idea she had so many friends. Well, some of them might be Owen's friends, too. She'd had no idea *they* had so many friends.

A shrill whistle cut through the noise. Patty. "Okay, everybody, let's hit the cafeteria! I'm starving."

"Sounds good." Owen slid his arm around Bailey protectively. "Isn't it clever the way I wangled a free engagement party?"

"With bear claws," she added. "Can we have those at our wedding, too?"

"We can have an entire bear if you want," he teased.

The rest of the evening passed in a happy blur. Afterward, Bailey was too tired even to think about packing, so she spent the night at Renée's. On Sunday, Ned showed up with a pickup truck. He and Owen and a couple of other guys moved her back to the house on Morningstar Circle, and they all celebrated with a pizza party.

Then, finally, Bailey spent the evening in Owen's arms, still trying to absorb the fact that he really, truly belonged to her.

To soften the media storm that Owen had feared, he and Bailey authorized Jennifer to issue a press release on Monday stating the basics of his paternity, the ways that she'd been ill-treated as a surrogate, their unexpected falling in love and their engagement. Understandably, Bailey refused to have anything to do with reporters, but Owen fielded questions when the press showed up.

He was pleased that the media reps, instead of acting nasty, seemed to relish the love story aspect. As for Phyllis, she apologized to her sister on the air but seemed miffed that Bailey had gotten engaged without telling her. Owen could only shake his head at the woman's arrogance.

To be on the safe side, he retained a family attorney on behalf of Bailey and himself. She assured him that, whatever games Phyllis or Boone might try to play in future, she would take steps to make sure the Storeys could never get their hands on the twins.

At work, the hospital buzzed with good feelings. On Thursday, when he and Bailey managed to eat lunch together, people kept stopping by with congratulations. "I feel like a celebrity," Bailey told him in wonder. "Guess you're used to it."

"I'm used to people respecting me, maybe admiring me," Owen conceded. "But not so much liking me."

"You're nothing like your reputation," Bailey told him.

"That's not entirely true. Let's just say I earned my bad rep the hard way, and now I'm un-earning it the easy way." Owen reached across the table to cup her hand. "Thanks to you."

"My pleasure." The joy radiating from her made him feel goofy and grateful all over again.

That afternoon, Owen was surprised to receive a call from Dr. Cole Ratigan, who had turned down the position of head of the men's fertility program. "Still got an opening? Winter's coming and I'm thinking it might be a lot more pleasant in California than Minnesota," the man said cheerfully.

"You bet." Elated, Owen filled in some details before

asking the obvious question. "To what do I owe this welcome change of heart?"

"Frankly, I hated turning down the chance to run part of your program, but I heard you were a real SOB to work with," Cole responded. "Now I understand you've turned into Prince Charming. I figure the truth has to be somewhere in between."

"I'm only an SOB on alternate Wednesdays," Owen said. "Good thing today's Thursday."

"I'll make sure to take Wednesdays off."

That was great news for their patients, for the program's reputation and for the fact that it gave Jennifer a new angle to release to the press. Owen sent her, Mark and Chandra emails, along with one to Alec Denny that probably wouldn't get read until he returned from his honeymoon. He and Patty had gone to Las Vegas to see the shows and indulge at the buffets.

There was one more thing Owen needed to do before he felt comfortable moving on with his life. Due to his tight schedule, it took until the following Saturday before he was finally able to visit his brother, who'd been returned to Southern California. Owen had to show ID at the jail, sign in and wait a couple of hours with a group that ranged from glum, gray-haired mothers and nervous young women to men sporting shaved heads and tattoos.

Behind a glass partition, Boone held himself tightly. The orange jumpsuit gave his skin a yellowish cast, especially the bruising around one eye.

"Saw you on the news," Boone said through the connecting phone, which they had been warned was monitored. "Good luck to you and Bailey. Guess I sort of played Cupid."

"Guess you did," Owen agreed. Now that he was here, he wasn't sure where to start. "Is there anything you need?"

"A get-out-of-jail-free card." Boone cracked a faint smile at this reference to their childhood games of Monopoly.

"Is there any way you can make this better?" Owen felt foolish asking, but he had to try. "If you tell them where the money is, maybe they'll cut you a deal."

Instantly, his brother's amusement vanished. "Is that why you're here? Did the prosecutors send you?"

Owen frowned, startled. "No. I've just heard you're facing a long sentence. And if the news accounts are true, you hurt a lot of people. Some of those seniors are in pretty desperate straits. I can't believe you…" He swallowed. *I can't believe the brother who protected me is capable of such self-serving evil.*

"The whole story hasn't come out yet," Boone responded smoothly. "Believe me, the prosecutors will be begging for my help. I have to be careful. You don't understand the pressure I've been under."

"From whom?" Owen asked.

"Now, I can't reveal that, can I?" his brother said. "You aren't here because of Bailey's chump change, are you? A big successful surgeon like you, I'm sure you're raking it in."

Vague references to secrets and pressure failed to persuade Owen that there were any mitigating circumstances. He might have tried harder to get through to Boone if not for that sneering reference to Bailey's hard-earned savings, as if Owen's presumed large income justified stealing from her. Clearly his brother felt no guilt whatsoever about cheating people who'd put their trust in him.

It reminded him of the excuses Boone's father used to

weave for disappointing his son and failing to pay child support. There'd always been someone to blame, and when their mother tried to pin him down, he'd kept changing his story. There had never been, not once, an honest admission of wrongdoing or a genuine attempt to set things straight.

Owen had come here hoping against hope that beneath that smooth exterior lay a conscience and a heart. He'd been wrong.

"Guess we're done here," Owen said. "Good luck to you."

"I never depend on luck. The trick is to be smarter than everyone else. You should know that."

"Oh, I'm not nearly as smart as I used to believe." *And neither are you.* "See you, bro."

"Thanks for visiting."

Leaving the jail with a knot of other grim-faced visitors, Owen knew he'd lost the brother he'd once loved. Lost him a long time ago, without realizing it.

But he was free, too. Had Boone shown even a glimmer of remorse, Owen would have felt obligated to keep trying to recover the stolen millions. He'd have bent over backward to help his brother redeem himself. And he understood now that it would all have been in vain.

"IT's IRONIC," BAILEY SAID that night as she snuggled next to Owen on the couch. She loved being back here and having the freedom to hug him as much as she wanted.

"What is?" He stroked one hand lightly over her abdomen, enjoying the twins' antics.

"Once you marry me, you're stuck with Phyllis as your sister-in-law, even after she divorces your brother."

Owen gave a rueful chuckle. "I hadn't thought about that."

"She called today. She wants to stay in touch, and she promised up and down never to make any claim on the babies again. Not that we're going to rely on her word for that." Although Bailey hadn't entirely forgotten or forgiven the events of the past few months, she hated being estranged from her sister. "I told her that I want Nora for my matron of honor, but I might let her be a bridesmaid. Along with Patty and Fiona, of course."

"Are you sure?" Owen asked. "After seeing Boone for what he really is today, I'm finding it hard to give either of them any leeway."

"I'm not stupid," Bailey told him. "I won't give her money and I'll never leave her alone with the babies. But eventually, she might meet a decent guy and lead a normal life, although if that happens, I may hire Patty to check him out."

To her relief, Owen didn't argue. "I used to think I knew best about everything. You've been teaching me otherwise since the day we met. So I'll leave your relationship with your sister to you."

"And I used to think you didn't have a heart," Bailey admitted. "Guess I learned a lesson, too." She let out a long breath. There was a matter she'd wanted to bring up since they got engaged, but hadn't found the right time. She wasn't sure this was it, but the longer she delayed, the more her conflict grew. "Owen, remember that I wanted to be a nurse practitioner? I realize that's not exactly a big goal compared to your career, and I don't have the money yet, but…"

To her dismay, he shifted her gently away from him, so she rested against the arm of the couch. "That reminds me. Hold on a sec."

As he swung away through the house, she wondered if she'd upset him. More likely, he hadn't been paying attention and was dealing with something else. The number one husband skill in her book was really listening to your wife. Obviously, he had a ways to go.

Back he came from the bedroom with a package wrapped in red paper and tied with a white bow. Judging by the dimensions, it might be a square candy box, but why make such a fuss?

"It's, um, very pretty," she said.

He placed it gently in her hands. "A special gift for my very special wife-to-be."

Growing more intrigued by the moment, Bailey tugged at the ribbon and finally got it untied. Then she slid her thumb along the tape to preserve the paper. Growing up in a penny-pinching household, she'd learned to reuse everything.

Owen was watching intently. A little embarrassed by her old habits, she reached inside the paper and pulled out...

...a first aid kit.

Bailey laughed. "I do need one of these. I have no idea what my sister did with the old one."

"Open it." Owen's tone implied there was something extra inside.

Curious, Bailey unsnapped the lid. Inside, atop the rolls of bandages and antiseptic, lay a small computer-printed certificate. It read:

As my wedding gift to you, I promise to pay for your education as a nurse practitioner whenever you're ready, and for any other training you might want. I also promise to put in extra babysitting, arrange for meals and, if you like, hire a nanny to make sure you have enough time for classes and study.

From the man who will love and cherish you forever.

She could hardly finish reading through the blur of tears. More than any flowery words or vague promises, this was proof that he not only loved her but also considered her an equal in their marriage. If she'd learned anything these past weeks, it was that no matter how the outside world might view them, they could only weather whatever storms the future might bring through genuine respect and a willingness to meet each other halfway.

Setting down the gift, she moved to his lap and wrapped her arms around him. "You are the most wonderful man in the world."

"I don't know if I qualify for that honor, but I'm willing to try," Owen responded, and kissed her tenderly

As he held her close—held *them* close, with the twins squirming at the pressure—Bailey felt her last reservation slip away. While most guys might not stick around, she knew from the bottom of her soul that the man she loved would be here tonight, and tomorrow, and for all the tomorrows to come.

She couldn't ask for anything more.

* * * * *

REQUEST YOUR FREE BOOKS!
2 FREE NOVELS PLUS 2 FREE GIFTS!

LOVE, HOME & HAPPINESS

YES! Please send me 2 FREE Harlequin® American Romance® novels and my 2 FREE gifts (gifts are worth about $10). After receiving them, if I don't wish to receive any more books, I can return the shipping statement marked "cancel." If I don't cancel, I will receive 4 brand-new novels every month and be billed just $4.49 per book in the U.S. or $5.24 per book in Canada. That's a saving of at least 14% off the cover price! It's quite a bargain! Shipping and handling is just 50¢ per book in the U.S. and 75¢ per book in Canada.* I understand that accepting the 2 free books and gifts places me under no obligation to buy anything. I can always return a shipment and cancel at any time. Even if I never buy another book, the two free books and gifts are mine to keep forever.

154/354 HDN FEP2

Name	(PLEASE PRINT)

Address	Apt. #

City	State/Prov.	Zip/Postal Code

Signature (if under 18, a parent or guardian must sign)

Mail to the **Reader Service:**
IN U.S.A.: P.O. Box 1867, Buffalo, NY 14240-1867
IN CANADA: P.O. Box 609, Fort Erie, Ontario L2A 5X3

Not valid for current subscribers to Harlequin American Romance books.

Want to try two free books from another line?
Call 1-800-873-8635 or visit www.ReaderService.com.

* Terms and prices subject to change without notice. Prices do not include applicable taxes. Sales tax applicable in N.Y. Canadian residents will be charged applicable taxes. Offer not valid in Quebec. This offer is limited to one order per household. All orders subject to credit approval. Credit or debit balances in a customer's account(s) may be offset by any other outstanding balance owed by or to the customer. Please allow 4 to 6 weeks for delivery. Offer available while quantities last.

Your Privacy—The Reader Service is committed to protecting your privacy. Our Privacy Policy is available online at www.ReaderService.com or upon request from the Reader Service.

We make a portion of our mailing list available to reputable third parties that offer products we believe may interest you. If you prefer that we not exchange your name with third parties, or if you wish to clarify or modify your communication preferences, please visit us at www.ReaderService.com/consumerschoice or write to us at Reader Service Preference Service, P.O. Box 9062, Buffalo, NY 14269. Include your complete name and address.

*Harlequin® Special Edition® is thrilled to present a new
installment in* USA TODAY *bestselling author
RaeAnne Thayne's reader-favorite miniseries,*
THE COWBOYS OF COLD CREEK.

*Join the excitement as we meet the Bowmans—four
siblings who lost their parents but keep family ties alive
in Pine Gulch. First up is Trace. Only two things get under
this rugged lawman's skin: beautiful women and secrets.
And in Rebecca Parsons, he finds both!*

*Read on for a sneak peek of
CHRISTMAS IN COLD CREEK.
Available November 2011 from Harlequin® Special Edition®.*

On impulse, he unfolded himself from the bar stool. "Need
a hand?"

"Thank you! I…" She lifted her gaze from the floor to
his jeans and then raised her eyes. When she identified him
her hazel eyes turned from grateful to unfriendly and cold,
as if he'd somehow thrown the broken glasses at her head.

He also thought he saw a glimmer of panic in those
interesting depths, which instantly stirred his curiosity like
cream swirling through coffee.

"I've got it, Officer. Thank you." Her voice was several
degrees colder than the whirl of sleet outside the windows.

Despite her protests, he knelt down beside her and began
to pick up shards of broken glass. "No problem. Those trays
can be slippery."

This close, he picked up the scent of her, something fresh
and flowery that made him think of a mountain meadow on
a July afternoon. She had a soft, lush mouth and for one
brief, insane moment, he wanted to push aside that stray lock

of hair slipping from her ponytail and taste her. Apparently he needed to spend a lot less time working and a great deal *more* time recreating with the opposite sex if he could have sudden random fantasies about a woman he wasn't even inclined to like, pretty or not.

"I'm Trace Bowman. You must be new in town."

She didn't answer immediately and he could almost see the wheels turning in her head. Why the hesitancy? And why that little hint of unease he could see clouding the edge of her gaze? His presence was obviously making her uncomfortable and Trace couldn't help wondering why.

"Yes. We've been here a few weeks."

"Well, I'm just up the road about four lots, in the white house with the cedar shake roof, if you or your daughter need anything." He smiled at her as he picked up the last shard of glass and set it on her tray.

Definitely a story there, he thought as she hurried away. He just might need to dig a little into her background to find out why someone with fine clothes and nice jewelry, and who so obviously didn't have experience as a waitress, would be here slinging hash at The Gulch. Was she running away from someone? A bad marriage?

So…Rebecca Parsons. Not Becky. An intriguing woman. It had been a long time since one of those had crossed his path here in Pine Gulch.

Trace won't rest until he finds out Rebecca's secret, but will he still have that same attraction to her once he does? Find out in CHRISTMAS IN COLD CREEK. Available November 2011 from Harlequin® Special Edition®.

Harlequin
Super Romance

Discover a fresh, heartfelt new romance
from acclaimed author

Sarah Mayberry

Businessman Flynn Randall's life is
complicated. So he doesn't need the
distraction of fun, spontaneous Mel Porter.
But he can't stop thinking about her. Maybe
he can handle one more complication....

All They Need

LONGER
BOOK
Same Price!

*Available November 8, 2011,
wherever books are sold!*

Discover two classic tales of romance in one
incredible volume from

USA TODAY Bestselling Author

Catherine Mann

Two powerful, passionate men
are determined to win back the women
who haunt their dreams...but it will
take more than just seduction
to convince them that this love will last.

IRRESISTIBLY HIS

Available October 25, 2011.